GIAUS

THE FERAL COURT, BOOK II

MYRA DANVERS

This book is dedicated to the swamp of tepid soup that has been my brain over the last few months. Really just a mess of fog and confusion that somehow turned into… this, a book that I am ridiculously proud of, no matter that I am just an "indie writer who has some raw potential but needs a polish and push in the right direction, but could stand to learn something about grammar before I can take the next step."
And also, to the Chaos.
The beautiful, endlessly spinning shit blizzard that is my life.
I would be nothing without the writing fuel.

Gleaming amber eyes fixed on his prize, the hunter watched from downwind. He watched as slender, female limbs were slowly stripped of the leathers keeping her hidden. Her clothing a shield that reeked of death and rancid fat, but beneath it all? The scent of breeding female.

His female.

The taste of her coated the roof of his mouth, etched in the lining of his nostrils. Scrawled in elegant pen along the inside of his skull, imprinted on his brain in a way that let him filter all else out. The complexities and subtle textures that were unique to her alone, committed to the hunter's memory. Obsessively focused on the one thing he wouldn't walk away from.

His mate.

At no point in his mad dash did the hunter stop to wonder *why*. Why this slight creature? A female of a species not his own, stained in the fluids of other males. Soiled. Used. Beautiful and wild.

He only knew that she'd been created for him. A gift of the Nine he'd forgotten to worship. A lure he couldn't refuse, and one he wouldn't allow to slip through his fingers no matter how many others had touched her first.

And so he watched as she dared to bathe when she should have been running, her lips frozen in a sharp grin with blunted teeth. Eyes over-bright with the sheen of victory.

Hunger pulsed through his veins. An itch to wipe that smirk off her face, to replace it with simple, enthralled adoration as she was remade to suit his needs. To worship all that he was.

To master this female whose wildling spirit had been fed by lesser males, left untamed.

The beat of his pulse throbbed along his girth, heavy and hot. Swollen with desperate, aching need. And yet, he had merely stalked her through the wood.

Watching.

He kept himself secreted away, downwind. Loping along at her back as she fled through the brush, planning as he hunted, as she put distance between her and the pack. Learning her scent, her limits.

Even now, with a vulnerable female exposing herself to his ravenous gaze, he contented himself with the show. Claws extended where they dented his palms, he lurked out of sight. Drinking down her scent in one deep lungful after the next, while she remained oblivious. Waiting so his prey might continue undisturbed, scrubbing those rejected pack males from her delectable skin, she prepared herself to be drenched in *his* scent. To reek not of death and fear, but of belonging. Ownership.

To him.

Unbidden, a growl rumbled through his diaphragm. Pert, reddened nipples exposed to watching eyes. Fingerprints marred her hips, arms, her neck and ribs. Evidence of the other males who'd had her first. How brutal their joining, how careless and greedy they'd been with so precious a commodity as this.

Hackles rising, the hunter sucked fury between clenched teeth. Exhaled a steady stream of hard-fought patience, for this female had proven herself a cunning warrior. One who wouldn't appreciate a simple, brutal fuck in shallow waters, but deserved the rigors of a proper taming hunt. She deserved to be worshiped with a chance to pit herself against a worthy suitor, to lose, only because she'd been bested and tamed.

Her match met, her place at his feet earned.

It was nothing less than what she deserved, to be broken over his cock, her primal needs serviced. Her appetite for rebellion smothered by a male equal to ruling her. Eating nothing, he'd let her feast on *him* as she was knotted and made to still. Her thirst quenched with what he'd pump down her throat. And then, when she'd been made to submit, when her eggs began to drop in honor of his conquering, he'd fill her belly with life. Take pleasure in watching her grow ripe with the evidence of his virility, she'd fast and beg for more.

Carefully hidden, he watched her shimmy free of the remainder of her clothing. Shucking putrid leathers on the sandy banks before plunging naked into the stream with a musical sigh.

And then she offered grave insult.

Fingers plunging beneath the surface, she scrubbed between her legs. Treating her abused flesh as if it wasn't the source of divine beauty that had drawn him in from leagues away.

He planted one hand on a tree trunk, claws sinking deep into the bark. Exerting himself to remain hidden in the shelter of shadows instead of charging into her life and fucking everything that was wet and wanting. Watching as her fingers delved between reddened thighs, as she plundered swollen tissue with deft movements, and cleansed herself of their leavings. Scoring her insides until that shallow stream was laced with the flavor most coveted in the Silver City and beyond it. Her slick flowing freely, despite a night of rutting with unworthy males.

The hunter stood sentinel through the rough ritual, seething, he guarded her against the legions of corrupted unworthy. Those who would slake their needs, their hunger, and leave her broken. Those who would reduce her to little more than a tribute to monsters reigning in the dark.

Plunging her head beneath the surface gave the hunter a moment's reprieve. A moment to vent the tension winding tighter and tighter through his core, his breath exploded from frozen lungs. Cock jumping where it hung fat with need.

Dripping and angry.

But it was only a moment. She popped back up with a dainty, feminine squeal. Purpled nipples tightened into points, gooseflesh pimpling every available hint of bared skin.

She was quick about dressing. Slipping into leathers with the sort of efficiency that spoke of an innate need for speed over comfort. Still wet, the leather squeaked where it was dragged over her limbs, concealing his prize once more. Her mop of dark hair was twisted and wrung free of excess moisture, bunched in a messy knot, then tucked beneath her hood. Kneeling, she brought a palm full of chilly water to her lips and drank deep, her gaze locked not on the dangers watching from the gloom, but the stream itself.

A fatal mistake born of inexperience, speaking of just how lucky she'd been to survive this long. For to expose herself like this, was to show herself to be a babe among beasts. An innocent, utterly ignorant of the true dangers that was life beyond the wall.

Unforgivable that she would be so bold. So careless with her safety.

A mistake he'd be sure to prevent her from making ever again.

She paused to stretch, thinking herself safe. That her only concern was the pack of males she'd claimed and abandoned. Her pace, when she once again took up her flight, was nothing short of leisurely. A stroll in the morning that took her right past his hiding place. Offering him a chance to inhale the breath she left in her wake, tiny feet landing within striking distance of where he'd hunkered down. Oblivious to the threat as she meandered by.

It was then, as she traipsed between shafts of dappled sunlight, that he caught a glimpse of her face.

Elegant, high cheekbones. Her jaw a sharp slash that blended with ears left mercifully intact, her form was pleasing. High-bred, all refined lines and exquisite curves. And there, hidden beneath leather, her hips set in a gentle flare meant to cradle his young. Hips that would fit in one hand. Fragile enough to crack, sturdy enough to bend when the demand was issued.

Unblinking, he watched her slip into the gloom. The quiet rustle of a small creature trying to go unnoticed. But he'd seen what lay clutched between her fingers. The little bits of forest fluff and pretty rocks her kind were known to hoard, her eyes glassy. Pupils blown wide and unseeing as she wandered. Searching and snuffling for more.

A slave to instinct, she'd abandoned the safety of her pack, thinking her needs had been met. Thrown herself to the mercy of an unforgiving place rife with predators slavering for the kill.

Her season still ripe.

Drawing in another lung full of her delicious scent, he filled himself with fury.

An explosion of sound ripped free of his chest. Setting the forest alive with startled creatures both hungry and small. Sleeping and waiting. They all fled from the sounds of the hunter declaring a challenge. Only the scavengers remained, circling high above, they watched with beady eyes. Knowing that sound was might be followed by easy pickings.

The girl squealed, branches and twigs snapping as she bolted from the brush without a thought toward discretion. Flushed out, she fled like the prey she was. His every sense triggered for the hunt. The chase.

The reward of wearing her down and filling her up.

Strides long and lazy, he paced her through the gloom. Driving the scent of terrified female toward the edge of the forest, where the hunting was effortless and relaxed.

An open space, with nowhere to hide...

2

Sleep clung heavy and languid to Balkazar's mind. The war chief resting comfortably, *warm* in a nest saturated with the scent of his prince, their pack, and a well-bred female. One they'd had together. One who'd mewled and begged, her mind utterly lost to her caste as she'd taken all they had to give.

Mindless little bitch had loved every second of it.

Enthralled to the gifts of her gender, she'd produced beautifully for her new masters. Her slick flowing in hearty abundance, just as it had been engineered to do. So she might entice the males born to rule her. Intoxicating them with every taste of the ambrosia flowing from between her legs. That this breeder was of the most cherished stock—worthy of

Hadim himself, before he'd cast her out—came as no real surprise.

Balkazar had never sampled her equal, but then, he was no prince born to inherit luxury.

Drunk on slick, depleted in the most satisfying way, the war chief had slept easily for the first time since they'd been exiled, docked, and mutilated. Slept and woken to the sounds of Sinadim taking her again in the small hours where darkness reigned. The prince's fingers wound tight in silken black hair as he pressed her into a nest she'd refused to build herself. Demanding to be submitted, despite the way she'd opened for them.

Resisting even as her back arched and her knees widened. Begging Sinadim for more, despite the knot ballooning inside her. Sealing his royal seed inside, the prince had been the last one to claim her. The anvil flare of his cock scrubbing her clean of competition, he'd left only his seed inside her. Deep as he could go. Marked by the pearly ooze of the most dominant male.

It was his right.

The heat of another twisted against Balkazar's hip. Squirming, the prickle of fine hairs teased his groin, and the war chief groaned. Taking a great, huffing breath, just to bring the memories rushing back. His vision filled with writhing flesh. Intoxicated, the two Anhur males had been selfish with their prize. Keeping the others from sampling that which they'd been born to covet, they drank her down until her eyes had gone glassy. Pupils blown so wide, she'd become little more than a vessel for Anhur sperm. One they'd over-filled before they'd allowed any of the hybrids to so much as touch the greedy girl.

Lounging in her pathetic nest, Sinadim had been content to watch the others defile her. Allowing her to suckle at his exhausted prick as one hybrid after the other mounted her from behind. Giving his brothers their due. Payment for their service, for they were not his kin. Not born with the compulsive loyalty that made those hybrid sons the envy of all unattached males. Instead, Sinadim paid them in a pussy dripping in slick, indulging himself in the show until he was ready to take her again.

And Balkazar? He'd been given free reign. Second only to the prince himself, the war chief had taken liberties that would have seen him hanged in the Silver City. Gelded for the crime of touching a precious harem breeder. Of daring to pump her womb full of unworthy seed, and endangering the bloodlines.

It hadn't stopped Sinadim before, when

they'd been in service to the Sultan, but here? In the wilds beyond the wall?

The prince was untethered by his father's morality. Free to revel in hedonistic delights of watching a female he'd claimed stretched out by another.

Since the very first time Sinadim had led Balkazar into the quiet gloom of his private, royal harem, Balkazar had known the prince to be generous in a manner other Anhur were not. And it was the prince himself who'd told him to sample one of his many treasured gems. The simpering little slut offered as a reward for a battle well-fought—the swelling of her belly, however? That one of the kits born moons later blinked up at him with the same blue irises he saw in the mirror?

It was a high he'd been chasing ever since.

Groaning, eyes closed, Balkazar stroked the plane of hard flesh lined up at his groin. The prickle of wiry hairs against his palm was one that saw a confused frown pinching the space between bunched brows.

Still, his erection pulsed with interest. The scent of what they'd done permeating his brain with memories, and the knowledge that no matter how exhausted, this new female was still in season.

She'd be ripe for days, yet.

Unable to be anything at all, except for willing. Eager for more until her *Biquea* glands were submitted and milked dry, her system flooded with the soothing balm to a natural season.

And this time, Balkazar didn't need permission to plant life inside her. Life that would reflect the quality of the dam they'd caught.

By the fires, the lengths she'd gone to lure them in! Feisty didn't begin to describe their pretty little breeder.

The Omega who'd laughed at a gentle touch.

Scoffed when the hybrids had been kind and hesitant with their prize.

Sneered when Sickle sought to offer her comfort, when the silly creature had tried to coo and set her at ease.

Balkazar had never seen such a thing before. A lowly Omega female, in heat, capable of setting traps and denying the commands of not one Anhur male, but two.

But when they'd finally gotten free of their bonds?

Gods, the way she'd fought! Hissing and spitting, their little breeder possessed the heart of an Anhur female, fresh from the fighting pits.

Even now, after emptying himself dozens

of times, the war chief needed more. Hips flexing, he ground himself against the heat of another. Finding his path already slippery, he stretched with a rumbling groan.

His dreams had been infected with the whisper of silky black hair matted with ropes of royal seed. Dreams in which the prince had been by his side, allowing him to take her first. Sinadim's shadowy presence spurring him on, imagined, ghostly fingers pushing him deeper into that spoiled, desperate cunt.

With a grunt, Balkazar's eyes snapped open. Hovering on the edge of orgasm, he found slender limbs pinned beneath his weight.

Limbs inked with the swirling designs of a Hathorian slave.

A male.

Sickle.

For one uncertain instant, as Balkazar scowled down at the boy, he considered the curve of plump flesh laid out before him. Not a warrior, the boy was soft where he was achingly hard. Ink twisted in elegant patterns over Sickle's back and ribs, the etchings of his Hathorian lineage scrawled down the bumps of his spine. And the scar of a docked tail that sat just above the pale crinkled flesh that lay hidden between smooth, lightly muscled cheeks. A hole that had surely been used before…

His cock dripped.

Snarling, Balkazar staggered to his feet. Eyes flicking over tangled limbs. Elbows and knees, broad shoulders and sparse manes—but no slender female among them.

Struggling to rise, he threw off a heavy forearm draped over his hip and, head tipped back, he took a breath.

Trying to follow her path from the nest, the scent of slick hung heavy in the still air, serving only to confuse his senses. Instead, he scowled at his surroundings, blue eyes searching the shadows, went back to the slumbering shapes of his brothers, seeking the curves that fit *just so* in the palm of his hands.

"She's gone," the prince said, voice a breathy rasp. Nothing more than a bulky silhouette against the mouth of their impromptu cave, his naked back tight with bunching muscles that spoke of his scarcely restrained fury.

"Gone?" Balkazar asked, a harsh bark of disbelief as he scrambled from the nest. Stepping on Micha's thigh, the dusky flesh dimpled beneath his foot. "How—"

Turning to face him, Sinadim's good eye flicked over the war chief. His good eye wild and rimmed in red. "The little bitch ran."

Heat rushed to Balkazar's cheeks. The flush of shame that crept over his nape and spilled across his entire face. Shame that she'd dare to offer such grave insult—and *after* she'd been properly claimed and submitted, no less. "Ah…" he sighed, glancing back to the pile of limbs tangled around each other. "A fuckin' shame, that. Stupid whore."

Dragging a breath between clenched teeth, Sinadim's hackles rose across broad shoulders. The scent of Anhur musk peppering the air with the flavor of his rage. But, with a howl, the prince whirled on *Balkazar*. Fists clenched at his sides, the Alpha male shivered with something beyond fury, a misplaced tempest. One working pupil narrowed to a tiny prick of darkness, the other fixed where it lay ruined and bisected.

And then, through the low rumble of a growl, his words shimmered to life. "Prepare the others to hunt."

"You mean to collect her?" Balkazar choked on a laugh. "She was a good fuck, I'll give her that. But"—he knelt, touching the tiny impression where her footprints led away from the mouth of the cave—"her trail's almost gone cold. She's had hours, Sinadim. Hours roaming the wilds, reeking of high-quality pussy. *In heat*." The war chief shrugged, his cock deflating against his thigh. "She's probably already dead. Her corpse being rutted by a hoard, even now—"

Lunging, Sinadim caught Balkazar's throat in his fist. Slammed him against the rock wall so hard his head cracked and his vision splintered. *"Don't,"* the prince spat, his every muscle vibrating where his heat pressed against Balkazar's nudity.

Gone was the sense brotherhood they'd found with a bitch spread between them. In its place, a prince shaking with a possessive rage the likes of which Balkazar had never known.

"Sinadim," the war chief said, swallowing when the prince's claws extended. Leaving marks against his throat. "My prince, you know I'm right. The girl is already dead—"

A shimmer of blonde fur shivered once as the prince pressed closer still. His gaze a horrific thing that whispered of vengeance. Of retribution against the truth. One eye a vibrant green, the other a flat, dull white. His face a mask of the grotesque, and in that moment, Balkazar saw what the girl had done to his prince. The obsession she'd wrought with nothing more than a dripping, sloppy quim.

The poison.

"You'd risk us all for *her*?" the war chief barked, shocked. Forgetting to fear the brother who'd given so much. That he wasn't merely an ally, but a former prince who'd run a massive harem. The First Born. Named and chosen to sit third in line to the Karahmet throne.

"*I* will rally the others," Sinadim whispered, his breath a furious hiss against Balkazar's cheek. His lips. "*You* will go ahead. Hunt her down and bring her back, Balkazar," the prince spat, leaving the rest unsaid. The promise of retribution for failure.

Despite the prince's temper, it wasn't rash, as far as plans went. Traveling with a pack—especially one bogged down with a pathetically soft Hathorian male—was slow going. Though several of the hybrids boasted a more refined sense of smell than either of the Anhur, their sheer size made fast travel impossible. Lumberous mutants that they were.

And Sinadim? The prince was half blind. Vulnerable, his lineage suited to being served. Issuing commands that were obeyed without question, not risking senseless death against a hoard of mindless infected.

No, Balkazar was the right choice, because Balkazar was *expendable*.

For an instant, as he submitted to Sinadim's claws, the war chief considered.

Calculated what it would take to overpower his Alpha… and take his place.

The thought had scarcely bothered to form before he shook it away. Hackles rising up on a wave of gooseflesh. But a whisper lingered, nevertheless. A sinister spark of something he couldn't completely ignore, no matter his love for the male whose grip had flexed about his throat in brotherhood *and* ownership.

Sinadim jerked his chin toward the exit. Saying nothing. Demanding everything.

And Balkazar obeyed, his pride bruised more than the fingerprints scored along his windpipe. Dressing with haste, the war chief said nothing as he rushed to leave, trying not to hear the harsh edge of madness in Sinadim's voice as he ordered the others up. Readying them to fly into the maw of almost certain death for a fucking breeder who'd dared to run.

Seething, Balkazar took off. Pausing only to glance over his shoulder—and so doing, saw her final insult.

There, smeared on the wall, was a single word written in slick. A signature.

Renegade.

Oh, yes.

He was going to enjoy making her scream…

3

A strangled cry ripped free from her throat. Heart skipping over her ribs hard enough to make her stumble. Shocked, her nape grew damp with terrified sweat. Fear soaking through her layers to permeate the wind in her wake.

She was being hunted.

Worse, she'd *been* hunted, stalked, and now she was being chased.

Not by Hadim, the cruel nightmare she'd escaped. Who'd been her master until he'd docked her tail and been made to watch as she slipped through his hated fingers forever. Leaving only four parallel scars tracing the inside of her arm—from pit to elbow.

Not by Sinadim and his pack of rejects. The males she'd left in a cooling pool of their own collective failure.

No, as if in retaliation for her open defiance, something crashed through the brush at her back. Moving at speed. Trailing her and making no effort toward discretion.

Because none was needed.

A second roar blasted through the thinning forest, this one laced with the lilting edges of mirth. Trumpeted victory fought and claimed before she'd even begun to flee in earnest. Before she'd been afforded a real chance to fight.

An earnest scream spilled over her lips, her spear nearly slipping from sweat-slicked fingers. A scream that was high in pitch, crackling with all the chaotic, terrified energy lashing at the back of her throat. Beating at her sternum, the backside of her pelvis, for there, just beyond the limit of her vision, she could see bright light.

The edge of the forest, where every last centimeter of protective darkness ceased to be.

Heart in throat, she tried to split to the left. Tried to veer off, away from where the forest grew too thin. She was met by the flash of claws. The heated puff of breath against her cheek, warming her unprotected nape, before the beast fell back once more.

She knew, then, what he was doing.

He was toying with her. Herding her toward the light.

But she didn't turn. Didn't grace the hunter with even the slightest glance, or broadcast her spine-bending terror—she merely lengthened her stride. Tucked her chin, ears flat, her shoulder bunching around pumping arms. Spear held tight in a white-knuckled grip, she pushed herself to the limit of her endurance, gaze narrowed. Her field of vision tunneled down to a narrow prick of light. Focused only on the next step, dodging trees that grew pro-gressively more slender. From ancient behe-moths, to spindly saplings, Renegade was pushed beyond anything that might be used for shelter. Any fleeting shred of sanctuary she might have sought, for beyond the forest's edge there was nothing. Barren, dimpled hills of limestone pocked by volcanic activity, but no *life*. Nowhere to hide. Nothing to use.

Nothing but certain death.

Without giving a moment's respite, a savage blow was struck.

Her right ankle swept out from beneath her, leveraged, and the hunter sent her tum-bling to the forest floor in a confused heap of limbs. Rolling over and over herself, she screeched once before her breath was stolen. Her ribs impacting the trunk of a sapling no thicker than her thigh.

A painful stroke of good luck, for with

thundering feet, the hunter was unable to stop on such short notice.

From her peripherals, she took note of the beast. His bulk, the sheer size of the behemoth that snarled as he skidded to a halt, claws flashing as he tried to snatch at her shoulder and missed.

Shaking, her ribs frozen where her wind had been squeezed from her chest, she crouched right there in the dappled sunlight of early morning. Trapped. Spear at the ready, clutched in a white-knuckled fist. Petrified and utterly helpless to do anything but look, she took him in. Watching as the hunter righted himself and turned—a stolen moment that couldn't last, but one that shocked her still, nevertheless.

A mess of shaggy dark hair speckled with mats and burrs, he was unkempt. Mangy and disheveled.

And *big.*

Easily the weight of two Anhur males combined, she might have taken him for a hybrid if it wasn't for the unmistakable scent that hung thick in the air between them.

Alpha.

Anhur Alpha.

Straight down to his marrow, the scent of pure, virile dominance seeped from his very pores. A menacing cloud of primal, possessive rage clung to the fibers of his tattered clothing as he remained still, glaring. Seemingly content to let her drink her fill, he took a huffing breath and mirrored her pose. One comically large fist planted between spread knees, he balanced on his haunches as clumps of matted fur lifted from his shoulders. Posturing for her, utterly saturated in pheromones that broadcast exactly what he thought of finding a lone Hathorian female in the woods.

His intentions outlined in the obscene girth tenting the front of ruined pants.

But it was his eyes that truly caught her attention. Gold. Streaked with green and flecks of chocolate. The mark of a feral infected with the Trax virus.

Without a second thought, she bolted. Mindless terror nipping at her heels, for after everything—all that she'd suffered at the hands of a species not her own—this was it.

This was where it ended.

Before it had ever truly begun.

From the start, she'd been doomed by the Nine. Promised to fall beneath rutting hips. All it would take was a single bite of infected teeth, and she'd become nothing more than a mindless feral, if she survived at all.

Keening, Renegade whined as her lungs heaved, her gaze turning back as she fled.

The Trax had marked him. *Deeply.* He was a mutant, his genes warped, his nature altered only half as much as his body.

And he was toying with her.

It was the insult, more than anything else. The look of inevitability burning in that heated, rotten gaze.

Was she to suffer defeat without a fight? She, who'd learned to thrive in the beyond? Who'd taken a whole pack of males, and slighted a Karahmet prince with a spark of callous joy flicking in her chest?

No.

Baring blunted teeth, she fought the rush of instinct begging for her submission, and turned to save herself. Short spear at the ready as she darted through the trees.

In answer, heavy, careless footfalls crashed through the gloom at her back, long legs devouring the distance she'd fought so hard to claim. And with a flash of heated breath on her nape, a palm landed between her shoulders.

Renegade stumbled, knees buckling beneath the weight of a single push. Palms skinned when she tried to brace, she went down with a breathless squeal. She hadn't the time to squirm before she was pinned face-down in the dirt. Her spear caught beneath her, pressed into the earth.

Useless.

Thighs wrenched apart, an impossible weight landed on her back, and he moved between her legs with sinister intent. The brush of cruel, massive hands kneading at her hips, taking liberties before traveling up. Over bruised ribs, and higher still.

Silent, the graceless brute pulled at her precious cloak. Ripping the seams at her right shoulder in one savage tug. She was stripped of her priceless garment soaked in deadman's fat. The very thing that had kept her hidden all these months, obliterated with a few callous moments of effort. Reddened arms the only evidence of her struggle.

Burying his fingers in her sweat-soaked hair, he forced her head to the side. An open mouthed kiss pressed to the spot between shoulder and jaw, his tongue darted out to taste the sacred place where a Hathorian male might leave a claiming mark.

"No!" Renegade gasped, shameful tears gathering at the seam of her lashes, she strained away. "By the Nine, *please*!"

But there would be no reasoning with this beast. No compromise or conversation, for the

Trax had taken his mind. If the myths were true, he would seek to satisfy his hunger. Torn between tearing her to shreds with teeth and claws until his stomach bulged on a feast of flesh, or... rutting her blind. Mindlessly fucking until Renegade was little more than a sleeve for his drooling cock.

Addicted to feral cum.

Sobbing, her fingers clawing at the earth, she tried to crawl to safety. No matter the rough hands pinning her flat, the scent of dominance invading her brain, or the thick bulge pressing against the outer curve of her thigh. She fought with all she had.

Great whuffing breaths traced the delicate slope of her neck, the hunter taking her in, making himself familiar with her scent on an intimate level reserved for a master and his harem slave.

The sharp ache of teeth shouldn't have come as such a shock. Shouldn't have made her squeal and go still beneath the weight of a monster whose blunt, Anhur teeth clenched around muscle and sinew. Pinching without breaking skin.

If she didn't know it to be impossible, she might have thought he was toying with her.

And by the Nine, it shouldn't have set her pussy clenching at the seam of her leathers.

Her base needs inflamed in an instant by nothing more than a show of force. Needs she'd seen to, only the night prior!

But there was no mistaking the gush of slick, the subtle way her spine arched where her tail might lift in invitation. Hardly daring to breathe, she lay petrified beneath him, aroused and terrified all at once. The meat of her shoulder caught, forcing her compliance for fear of finding herself marked. Infected.

A growl rumbled against her skin. Starting low, she felt it first against her spine. Where he'd stripped her of her cloak and left her in a sweat-soaked undershirt. It traveled up, rattling between her ribs, injecting her heart with pure, primal fear until there was nothing else. Only the sound of the largest male she'd ever encountered, preparing to mount her. The rut a heavy curtain of threat and debauchery that hung over them both. His weight heavy across her back, one she couldn't lift. Couldn't fight.

Breath puffing against her ear, whistling through his nostrils, he exhaled. Released her skin without placing a mark, but paused to snuff at her nape.

He licked her, then. Low growl growing sharp, his tongue rasping as it moved from shoulder to earlobe. Leaving a trail of goose-flesh in its wake.

Renegade whined, a pathetic, brittle sound that warbled around a sob. A desperate plea for mercy answered only by the press of hips, the threat of violence that pulsed against her lower back. Once, twice—and then he was gone.

Gasping, her every muscle trembling, she twisted and found the hunter balanced on his haunches once more. Simply watching her. One hand pressed to the dirt between spread knees, the other working at the laces keeping his ragged pants about his hips. Tongue making a scandalous pass across full lips, he caught her gaze in his. Held her there for a moment, until she managed to scramble back with a vicious curse. Heart pounding. Breath coming short and wild, as she stared back at golden amber eyes. Bewildered.

He grinned, displaying strong, white teeth.

Because he *wanted* her to run.

Wanted to hunt.

Renegade didn't need telling twice. Didn't need time to think of the chances that she might escape unscathed, she merely scrambled to her feet without a second glance, snatched her spear, then fled into the gloom.

4

Running and dipping, the lithe female sprinted as fast as her slender Hathorian limbs could carry her. Fleeing what she could not escape, the scent of his mate liberated from the confines of that putrid cloak soaked in fetid slime.

Pacing her, *easily*, the hunter loped along at her back. Admiring the way her muscles moved beneath her skin, the way tendons and sinew worked in tandem along the flat planes of her shoulder blades. Her skin *just* peeking through the tattered remains of an ill-fitting undershirt, while tangles of river-damp hair streamed along behind her.

Grinning, his mane standing on end where it wasn't plastered to his shoulders, he snarled at her just to hear her sing. Just to watch her feet stumble as she fought his claim, gorgeous dark eyes rimmed in dread, her gaze flicked back. That silly little spear clutched tight to her chest. Her ears laid flat, hidden beneath a curtain of wet hair, her lips parted around a panting, silent scream.

Entranced by inevitably, she squealed as she ran. Whatever she saw on his face held her rapt, her spine twisted as she looked up at him.

Running blind.

The hunter huffed, then stooped. Thundering feet never missing a beat, even as he reached out and caught her back ankle. Angling her away from the trunk of an unforgivingly large tree, he sent her spinning once more.

Tumbling over and around herself, she dropped the silly spear and managed to slow her fall with outstretched hands. A dainty yelp torn from her lips as she caught the bark of a fallen log then rolled, landing flat on her back.

She blinked up at the canopy above.

Dazed.

With a gleeful snarl, he pounced. Landing above her, balanced on the balls of his feet, he surged forward. Hands planted on either side of her slender neck, he braced. Teeth bared around a wild grin, panting, heating her cheeks with gusts of exertion. Arousal. Waiting for her gaze to clear, for the flames of her temper to catch and spread, pressed close enough that he could see it.

But he remained silent as he lingered. Content to watch and wait. The urge to growl —to assert himself and take possession—was caught and held behind gleaming white teeth.

She blinked. Parted lips sagging until she sucked in a breath, the girl came alive in an instant. Thrashing inside the cage of muscle and throbbing testosterone, kicking and screaming, she set blunt teeth to his forearm but couldn't offer more than a pretty bruise. One he would cherish, his cock pulsing at the thought of *real* claiming marks laid into his flesh. The rumors of a Hathorian mating bond something he'd long fantasized about.

Her most precious gift. One he would earn, no matter the cost.

By the Nine, he'd ensure *those* marks festered and scarred.

Releasing his forearm, she pressed her palms against his chest and shoved. "Get off me!" she shrieked, panting through an open mouth. Her energy already beginning to wane as she wasted it trying to lift an immovable weight.

He caught her wrist, pressed his nose to the spot where her skin had been scraped raw in her fall, speckled with little dots of beaded crimson. And then, meeting her gaze, he laved her palm from wrist to fingertips. Tasting the ambrosia of a female made just for him.

With a gasp, her pupils narrowed to tiny pricks of black and she snatched her wrist back. Cradling her bleeding palm to her chest, she slapped him with the other.

For a moment, he was still. Cheek tingling, he could feel the outline of each tiny finger. Her palm and the outrage she'd branded him with. But he did nothing in retaliation. Merely pinned her there with the weight of his glare, surprised that a Hathorian would dare.

Delighted by the sheer perfection of the creature beneath him.

"Get off me, feral," she hissed, the rumbling coo of a feminine growl offered in place of apology. Her knees brought up, tucked between them as she readied herself to throw him off. And then her features grew hard. Determined and fierce, she spat, "You are unfit," through clenched and blunted teeth.

He blinked, just the once. The only metric of his surprise a shiver of his mane. An unseen twitch where he'd grown swollen with need, the pulse of lust hammering at his restraint. But still, he clung to that control, savoring the challenge offered by a female who had nothing. Not even her adorable pointed stick. Her nostrils pinched white, he took a breath just to know the depths of her fire. Painted her scent along the roof of his mouth, where he could taste it, the rich bouquet of breeding hormones and *her*.

His mate.

It wasn't enough.

With a surge of muscle, he caught her about the throat and cut off her squeak of protest. Clasping fingers an unspoken warning, he tipped her head to the side and drank her in. Face dipping low, his nose dented the delicate blue flutter trapped just under her skin, where a vein lay distended and healthy. Trapped and wriggling beneath the press of his thumb.

He drew in another ragged breath, took her in all the way down to the bottom of his lungs, where he'd never be rid of her. Ignoring all her attempts to heft him back, unconcerned by her flimsy claws trying to shred his thick skin or that her face was beginning to purple, he took his time.

Savoring her.

Licked at the spot that made her clench and mewl. Tasting the lingering evidence of her season, that she'd been bred thoroughly but not nearly well enough—her eggs not yet enticed to drop. Utterly taken by the prickle of delicate vertebrae against his palm, that so fragile a creature was his to do with as he pleased.

But still, she fought. Squirming and struggling despite the truth of her helplessness, she raged against his chest. Spine thumping back against the forest floor.

She wouldn't yield. Not when her eyes grew glassy and pounding fists landed with ever-lessening force, she refused to submit. Utterly so. He could see it etched between her brows. The crease at the edge of her lips, in bared teeth and flattened ears.

Defiant against all reason or sense.

Beautiful.

With a final, lewd inhale, he released her. Shoved her folded knees out of his way, and moved to cover her. To sit back on his haunches, a tiny fraction of his weight balanced on her hips—her legs rendered useless behind him. He left her free to kick and fight and waste the last of her energy, if it made her feel powerful.

His little warrior.

Only when she met his gaze did he offer her a taste of his intentions. Capturing her wrists, he stretched her out and pinned her arms high above her head. Breath caught, fingers hooked under the collar of her shirt, he pulled. Tore the wretched garment down the middle and exposed the full curve of her breasts, eyes catching on the twin peaks of nipples purpled by careless fingers.

Panting as she railed against him, she arched. Displaying all that she was for his perusal. His vision filled with swaths of pale skin bruised by dozens of fingerprints—none of them *his*. Marks left on her hips, her ribs, and there, beneath the scent of a female in season, he caught the scent of inferior males.

Their claim weak, but left to linger.

A growl echoed up, surging with a will of its own as he stared.

Free hand finding his laces, vibrating with possessive fury, he pulled his cock forth with no ceremony whatsoever. Pumping that engorged length, he shivered. Glare fixed to the hint of fresh bruises he would soothe with his essence. An unspoken oath of protection, he would bathe her in his scent so all might know this tiny, glorious female was not to be touched lest they invoke his wrath.

She groaned, the sound not that of a terrified female to be coerced into compliance, but of tortured denial. Her eyes black with need, pupils blown wide, she flexed. Straining to look, to catch a glimpse of the girth pumping and weeping between his fingers.

She wanted this. Recognized who he was, whether she wanted to admit it or not.

Glee sparkled up his spine, and he shifted to his knees. Milked his cock *just* out of sight.

Denying the little female not for her own good.

But for *his* pleasure.

Enraged, she bucked. Suffused with a rush of furious energy, she hissed and spit. Her temper serving only to spur him on. To make his prick seep, lubricating his fist as he worked. Forearm burning with the flash of effort, ass flexing and clenching in time with every upstroke, his thighs clenched about her middle. Pinning her there in the dirt, he paused only long enough to knead her soft, fatty swells. Released captured hands to pinch and tweak nipples already bruised by lesser males.

First the left, then the right. Rolling that beaded flesh between forefinger and thumb just to make her squirm. Back arching into his touch, her belly rubbed against his heavy balls.

Lips twisting around a grunt, he clenched his fist and returned to himself. Enthralled by the desperate needy thing laid out for his enjoyment, his fist working furiously out of sight. The only audible sounds were that which squelched between his fingers.

Until she whined, tears sparkling along her

lashes, she writhed. Caught in a cage of denial, her breasts lifted as she attempted to entice. Her training as a breeder settling in and taking over.

A low growl rumbled forth, so deep it was felt rather than heard. An echo of a voice he hadn't heard in... years. A voice he didn't recognize, though the unspoken command saw his female settled. Soothed. Helpless to deny the male who took his time to toy with his meal before he began to feast.

Such control when she was ripe and fertile, her body begging to be mastered and spread? It couldn't last.

"Please," she whispered, quivering. Her hips tilting back, her abs kneading his sack where it sat ripe and taut. Heavy with unspent seed.

He shuddered above her. Sucking a breath between clenched teeth, his eyes fixed not to jiggling flesh, but the bottomless black of her gaze.

And then, without prompt, she twisted her neck to the side. Exposing her throat as she might to a Hathorian male who wished to mount her. As she might to a lover... her mate.

With an ear-splitting roar, he succumbed. Splashing her nipples and belly in hot ropes of cum, he spilled, coating her skin in pearly strands of seed. Each rope landing with the lash of one marking dominion, it was more than skin deep. Bristling with each jet of seed left to mark her rosy skin.

Eyes losing focus, fucking his fist, the hunter laid his claim. Hips rocking as he peppered the still air with the sweet scent of virility.

A mewl beneath him brought him back from the edge. Fist still pulling at overwrought flesh, he milked every last drop onto her belly, then let his girth slap down into the mess. His cock left to deflate where it lay heavy and hot against her bellybutton, inching back toward twitching balls.

Rumbling, he scooped up a palmful of spilled cream and worked it into her bruises. Kneading it into her flesh until his palm grew tacky and that seed began to cool.

Only when her skin began to tug and stick to his palm did he relent, moving instead to pluck at one neglected nipple before he rolled to the side. Heart hammering away at the back of his throat, he let her stagger to her feet. Watched as she collected her spear and tried to knit the edges of her ruined shirt. His gaze hooded. Lazy. Tugging at his girth, her dizzy hesitation a pleasing sight, for he knew just what it was that marred those delicate Hathorian brows.

Knew what it was she wanted from him...

But it lasted only a moment. A brief flash of indecision before she lunged toward him with the gleam of madness in her eyes. Spear held aloft.

A single, cold bark of laughter left his lips an instant before he caught it with his off hand. Wrenching it from her grip with an ease that made her yelp, he didn't bother himself to inspect the deadly weapon. Merely tossed it aside and watched her bolt into the gloom once more, exposed, glazed tits bouncing with every step. The ruined flaps of her miserable shirt dancing in her wake.

Grinning, the hunter tucked his bloated length away and stood. Stretched out his back, rolled his neck, and filled his lungs with the sweet taste of a battle won. The first of many he'd dominate this day.

For pleasing him so well, he gave her to the count of thirty before he resumed the taming hunt.

The spear left forgotten where it jutted straight from the trunk of a tree.

5

Pressing at the stitch in her side, Renegade ran with her torn shirt. Bared and spattered with the seed of an infected Alpha, she gasped at the sound of thundering feet trailing in her wake. That he allowed her to attack without immediate retribution? To make a bid for safety at all, hopeless though it was?

It was a sign of the truth.

A thing she could no longer deny.

Because she knew this hunter was enjoying himself, enjoying the chase.

Her ruined shirt caught on a branch, tangling and jerking her awkwardly to the left. Arms wind milling, she tore free of the garment. Snarling and sweating, her hands trembling, she tried to free herself before he was on her again. Refusing to give up, no matter how likely her fall.

The gleam of golden eyes through the gloom mocked her as she stripped. As she whirled and crashed through a bramble, her skin torn with lashes and thorns. Moving before the pain could fully register, she sprinted. Topless. Disarmed. Maintaining a pathetic lead, she knew it wouldn't be long before she felt yet another blow meant to trip her up. That he'd close the gap between them when he grew tired of this game, force himself into the deepest part of her, and plant his mark in her belly.

Feverish, Renegade squealed. Horrified by the looming loss of her autonomy. Her choices no longer hers to make, she'd be left to bear the consequences. Left to live or die at the whims of the Nine when this infected beast grew weary of the pleasure he would wring from her cunt.

Fate threatening to seep through her resolve, Renegade did the only thing she could. Searching *not* for a den where she could hide, she looked up. Amongst the trees for temporary safety, a moment of peace where she could catch her breath. A place with a view of her impending doom.

Sobbing at the sight of a worthy candidate,

she leapt, catching the lowest branch of the closest tree in palms made raw for the amusement of a beast. She hauled herself up, kicking legs a poor counterbalance, her spine flexing where the phantom of her tail ached to work. Her hands trembled with the flush of terror pounding through her veins.

A snarl chased her higher still. Ringing with surprise, the hunter's voice an ancient rumble of displeasure she could feel rattling through every one of her vertebrae. Right down to the new base of her spine that itched and pulled. The nerves raw.

Fingers slipping, the leaves shimmered above her. A kaleidoscope of jewel tones that danced as she climbed, hauled herself up and over, then flung herself toward the next branch above.

And the hunter let her go.

He stood sentinel, head cocked, gleaming amber eyes fixed to her back as she evaded his reach. It wasn't until she'd scrambled over the third branch that she dared to take a breath. Arms wrapped around the trunk, her ribs clattered with the hysterical urge to giggle. Her tears ran in steady drips, cheeks tracked with dust and dirt. Nipples that had merely been bruised, were now chafed from where she'd dragged herself over rough bark, stinging where the salty tang of feral semen had been massaged into her skin. Raw scrapes reddened her belly and hips, everywhere hard edges were no longer protected by her precious cloak. Her undershirt.

Pacing below, the hunter circled her perch. Amber eyes gleaming from a demonic mask, lips peeled back from blunt teeth, he roared again. The sound threatening to burst her ear drums as she clung to temporary safety. Arms and legs wrapped around living wood. Eyes squeezed shut. Ears tucked, her bladder threatening to purge itself in a helpless sign of submission.

Hathorian submission, for it was nothing less than what she'd been bred to do when confronted by a male such as this.

An Alpha in his prime. One that wanted to possess what she was. Wanted access to her genetics so he might breed an army and reign supreme.

It was what they *all* wanted. Each and every one.

Above her, a high-pitched coo trilled an alarm, and her eyes snapped open.

She was met with a flash of azure. A tiny creature whose blink was reptilian, whose eyes consumed most of an angular, petite skull. No bigger than twice the length of her forefinger, its mouth lined with glass needles. Instead of forearms, it stretched wings tipped in sharp claws, and flexed two tails where it hung inverted. Wrapped around a branch, watching. Head twisting back and forth, the trill of curiosity warbling in sync with its movements.

And then she did cackle. The sound reedy and dry, making the winged lizard coo in sharp alarm. Six eye stalks rose from bony ridges as it came fully awake, glaring at the Hathorian female who'd dared disturb its slumber.

She'd never seen one this close, though she knew exactly the sort of creature she'd stumbled across. Knew they lived in great, hypnotizing flocks and dined in enormous numbers.

The hunter roared again. Rattling her bones and eardrums before he struck her tree with clenched fist, working to turn her sanctuary into kindling.

A thousand winds spread, then. Tiny colorful creatures hissing and trilling in sync. The tree itself was dead. Brittle. Nothing more than a perch filled with a flock of the tiny, ravenous creatures.

Renegade didn't waste another moment. She reached for the closest, snatched it from its perch, then hurled it down.

It sailed through the air with a shriek of

outrage. Twisting and turning as if in slow motion, the tiny creature tried to right itself. Wings flapping, tails lashing about. It sliced through the air—until the hunter struck it with a careless backhand.

With a crunch, it spun in the opposite direction. Quite dead.

But Renegade spared no remorse for the tiny life she'd sacrificed.

She grabbed another.

Scrambling up, she began to pluck living missiles at random. Her fingers closing around slender bodies with razor-sharp edges, she chucked them at the hunter as fast as she could catch the sleepy things. Palms scored by sharp teeth, claws, and two bony blades protruding from the tips of their split tails.

Dodging and weaving, the hunter's lips were no longer creased in triumph. Amber eyes had lost their possessive gleam, only to be replaced with a crackling blaze of fury.

Renegade hissed, showing blunted teeth. Her ears flat in blatant disrespect, and if she had a tail, it would be held stiff and aloft. Bristling with contempt.

It was all she had left. The flock of flying reptiles her only ally in a ravenous place that would never stop testing her will to survive.

She reached for the branch above her head,

feet careful, if clumsy as she crested another rung in her makeshift ladder. And this time, she reached for a tiny lizard still coated in the flaking black skin of youth. A creature too young to shed its camouflage to reveal the color it would bare throughout life.

As if cooperating with the beast below, her next throw sailed through the air and landed in the center of the hunter's palm.

Absurdly thick fingers closed over the adolescent that squealed and thrashed, and without so much as a blink, he brought that offering to his lips…

… and crunched through flesh and bone.

For one blistering instant—as the hunter chewed then tossed the bottom half of the adolescent aside—there was little else but silence. Nothing but the sound of the breeze, for the flock of lizards had gone still. Those in flight pausing to hover above the scene of carnage playing out on the ground. Still others hung from their branches. Drowsy. Blinking.

But as one, their soft cooing began to wail of vengeance. A call for revenge on the wretched beast that would dare attack a hatchling.

Entranced, Renegade dared a smile as the entire flock took wing, forming a murderous cloud that swirled around the hunter's filthy head.

At first, he hardly bothered to glare. His attention fixed on the unruly Hathorian he thought to claim, he wrapped both hands around the base of her tree and looked up. Ignoring the flock, teeth flashing with a bastardized smirk born of mirth and greed, he pushed. Bending the tree as far as its flexible young trunk would allow, he sent her tipping precariously toward the earth.

And then three things happened all at once.

With a unanimous cry, the flock of bejeweled lizards dove. Spitting their acidic breath in a great wet cloud of seething hatred that sizzled where it spattered. Making the hunter's skin hiss and char and smoke.

Distracted at last, the hunter roared in outrage. In pain. A challenge issued and answered before he'd finished that breath. Answered by a legion of tiny winged beasts that swarmed into one ravenous firebrand unafraid to attack a creature a thousand times the size of the individual.

And then his grip on her tree slipped. His effort to dislodge her abandoned as acid rained down on hunched shoulders.

Green wood bucked, snapping back with

force enough to compromise her stranglehold on the tree trunk. Launched from the safety of her perch, the velocity sent Renegade rocketing through the air. Shrieking at the top of her lungs, flung clear over the edge of the forest, she landed *hard*. Her knees buckling as she rolled. Dazed.

From her peripherals, she watched the hunter fight the deadly cloud with a fury that rendered her still, struck dumb at such a display of Anhur strength. His reflexes quick enough to see every mighty swing killing dozens of lizards with every swipe.

He wouldn't be distracted for long.

It was a struggle to stand. Her lungs seized in a frigid fist, her muscles begged for relief. To simply lay down and accept her fate.

Teeth clenched, she staggered toward open, barren planes. Limped toward the desolate, pitted field of limestone. To where she could see geysers steaming, belching up sulfurous smoke. And there, amongst the pools of bubbling water rimmed in crusty yellow foam, she could see darkness that tunneled down, and knew it to be a cave system carved by eruptions of volcanic fury.

Renegade couldn't help the terrified little squeal that burst from her lips as she fled from a monster. Couldn't help the tremor in her hands or stop her thoughts from turning to Sinadim and the pack of males she'd rejected.

But it was too late to call for help.

Too late to turn back and beg forgiveness, accept her place in a new harem, and breed for another male in the Karahmet line.

There was nothing but the limestone tunnels and the delirious hope that she'd found a place where the hunter couldn't follow.

6

S watting the air as the flock of *Volans* dove, he couldn't help but grin. Despite the sting of acid raining down on his shoulders, that it burned and bubbled. No matter the dozens of tiny bites sawing through his skin, feasting on blackened flesh, his smirk only grew.

She was glorious.

A creature born of his deepest fantasies.

Resourceful. Fierce and strong, her spirit indomitable.

A perfect match, in contempt of her inferior species. Hers was a fire he would tame but never extinguish, for her submission at his feet was a guarantee.

The Hathorian to his Anhur.

Helpless but to take yet another enthralled glance, he turned his attention up, toward the little female defying his unspoken commands. Teasing his patience with her coy games.

She was gone.

The tree was a barren shell with dead branches. Absent any hint of one insolent Hathorian whose scent had sent him spiraling into madness. Abandoning all sense in his quest to claim the beguiling little thing for himself.

Whirling, the hunter's eyes flicked through the gloom, his heart racing. Veins growing thick with the flush of adrenaline, his mane standing in defiance of the matted filth. The mud. Cracking free in a shivering bristle that reeked of possessive fury that she would dare—

His frantic gaze caught on a pathetic figure limping beyond the forest. A slender silhouette framed against a stark, desolate landscape, she was exposed. Out in the open, utterly vulnerable to attack, she staggered *toward* danger as if she had no idea where it lurked. Oblivious to the monstrous fiends who'd claimed the domain of dank, putrid sulfur fields.

And she was heading straight for the tunnels worming through limestone.

Throwing their playful game, the hunter exploded into motion. The flock of *Volans* fluttered above his head, forgotten for the nuisance they were. Claws extended, muscles surging, it took him fifteen strides to clear the tree line.

It wasn't fast enough.

With dawning horror, he watched the menacing form of a fire-kin emerge from its den. Frill fully extended, coiled and ready to strike, it was a fully mature female. A drake flecked with the pockets of white-hot flames for which the species had been named, her skin shimmered with embedded heat. With the blazing glow of a creature whose veins were filled with the very breath of the Nine—the sizzle of molten rock waiting to be unleashed on any threat deemed worthy of the effort, for the fire-kin ate their meat charred.

And his female had been disarmed.

Bellowing, the hunter charged. Ground-eating strides thundering against stone, he threw in a bid to distract one of the most deadly creatures living in the beyond. Ignored the startled look reflected in his mate's luminous black eyes, and snarled instead at the fire-kin. Intending to take her explosion of matronly fury upon himself, and spare the Hathorian who would know what it was to make amends.

The slight, foolish little bitch who staggered *toward* a drake at the sound of his challenge.

Put off an easy meal by the sounds of another apex predator in her midst, the fire-kin's gleaming eyes snapped to his face. Pupils a thin, alien slash of spite.

And in an instant, the hunter knew this would be a true battle.

Knew his mate had managed to find herself a *massive* female whose skin was speckled with the muted color markings of one guarding a clutch.

Ribs that should have been shielded under thick layers of scales and dense hide had grown jagged, the outer layer of skin sloughing off in great, flaking sheets. She'd been left ravaged by her brood, thin and ragged. Decrepit, yet more dangerous than any other time in her life cycle, for starvation had only made her lighter. Faster and vicious. Hormones had long blinded her to anything but the protective instincts that put her hatchlings above all else, fire-kin motherhood was to forgo food that didn't run directly into their gaping maw.

And his mate was shuffling too close.

Staggering.

Her gait that of wounded prey.

Racing against the cruel twist of fate, the

hunter's vision tunneled on his target. That the Nine would deliver her *here*, beyond the wall. Untouched by the ravages of so hard a life, only to sacrifice her to the belly of a mindless beast?

He wouldn't allow it.

Shoulder dropping, he launched himself between his mate and her doom. Sailing through the air, braced to land on the balls of his feet. The impact rippling through coiled muscles, he struck the instant he had the purchase to do so. Ignoring the searing heat, the sting of noxious fumes wafting from reptilian skin, he caught the beast behind one great, crimson frill and twisted. Driving its skull toward the earth in a bid to crack it wide open and lay its corpse at his female's feet. To end this now, quickly. Before the lava-kin could retaliate with a weapon far more deadly than any he had in his arsenal.

A warbling tri-toned cry pierced his ears, sent his brain jiggling inside his skull with nowhere to hide from a sound that wasn't. A sound that heralded annihilation for so many, the lava-kin merely blinked at the assault. Hardly bothering to be dazed, it simply flexed that thick neck and bucked the hunter off, then began to vibrate with a sub audible hum. The speckling of its hide going from white to an incandescent blue heat in an instant.

The lava-kin gagged—the only warning of what was coming.

Projectile vomit.

A splash of vibrant blue that began to cool as soon as it landed, burning through whatever it touched. Hot enough to melt through the rock, it reeked of sulfur.

It was all he could do to dodge in time. His survival a testament to unnatural reflexes unmatched by any Anhur living or dead. Spinning, he knocked his female clear with a backhand that sent her flying. Bruised but breathing. Her black eyes rimmed in white as she watched, staying where he'd put her down. Shocked dumb and still by the violence unfolding before her.

Whirling, the hunter crouched low. Braced and ready. His gaze fixed to the reptile rumbling a low warning, warbling back and forth. Pinning him first with the left, then the right eye. Oscillating back and forth, back and forth.

Taking one step to the left, the hunter met that primordial glare with one that matched. Seething. His every careful movement designed to distract away from the Hathorian female cowering in his shadow. The easy meal *he'd* be devouring at his leisure.

When he'd managed to turn the beast far enough away, he feinted. A sharp movement meant to bait. An offered decoy of the biggest target.

Again, the lava-kin's chest began to vibrate. Sound beyond hearing reverberating through his sinew, her chest flaring a sinister blue. His very cells danced to a tone he couldn't define, but was warning all the same.

The lava-kin retched again. This time aiming high, at the bulk of his chest.

He ducked.

Rolled.

Struck at the soft spot beneath her chin with claws fully extended, and came away burnt. His fingertips blistering upon impact with a beast born of magma, dealing devastating damage nevertheless. Claws singed, pocked and marked, but still intact enough.

The fire-kin staggered. Her jaw hanging loose where he'd wrenched it free of its hinge. Tongue lolling out, bile shimmering blue with intense heat dripped freely to the limestone. But instead of retreating, the fire-kin reared up. Standing on stocky back limbs, balanced on the base of a thick tail, her frill pulsed an angry red.

Chest emitting a near-constant thrum of warning, she lunged and hurled. Dodged and spit. Creating a minefield of molten stone as the hunter evaded.

Constantly driving attention away from his mate, he pressed any advantage he might glean. Drew back when life or limb were at risk, and rushed at any chance to land a blow.

There was no margin for error. No chance of brushing it off, should he be struck by so noxious a projectile. He'd be dragged into a den by a brood mother doomed by mortal injuries, yet too stubborn to give up her vigor. He'd be fed to her young while she watched on. Dying, so her body might feed her offspring. A final gift of her blood and bone.

He'd never know what it was to breed his female. To lock inside her and mark her as *his*.

The very thought had the hunter howling in contempt. Limbs working together, his balance a thing of deadly precision, he launched himself at the drake. Taking a swipe with his compromised claws before flying back. Offering a bluff to the left, and striking at the right, he tore at her hamstrings with a touch light enough to spare his digits from igneous gore. Pleased by the sounds of agony trumpeted from that deadly throat.

A whimper shattered his attention.

The plaintive cry of a female already

etched inside his skull, more than enough to impale his brain with a deadly splinter. An unforgivable instant of weakness.

She was just there. The reason for his fight tucked around herself as if being small was any less appealing to ravenous swine. Arms wrapped around her knees, her ears flicked back, she huddled in the mouth of a tunnel. Keening. Her terror a palpable thing born of the helplessness of her kind.

Looking not at the drake, but at *him*.

Something collided with his ribs. A blunt force trauma landing with enough violence to send him careening into stone, his head striking with a clatter that robbed his senses. Fractured time. Distorted light and stripped precious seconds from his memory.

With fetid breath, the lava-kin was on him. Everything and more to fight for, the brood mother would give her life for her young. Already had, though she meant to deliver him to the Nine herself. Crushing weight flattened his ribs beneath a clawed forelimb. The caustic spatter of bile missing his face by sheer blind luck that wouldn't last.

Feet drawn between them, he prepared himself for the last moments of the fight.

His trophy waiting to be claimed.

Ignoring the heat with enough intensity to

cremate, he let his claws become talons and sank his grip through flesh that burned. Shoved with both feet, and tore that throat free of its moorings. Avoiding the worst of it, he rolled away only half as fast as he should have. His hip and thigh scorched in reprimand. Branded by his effort, yet rewarded with the wet spatter of gore that signaled victory.

Tongue lolling through a gaping hole, the lava-kin took three mincing steps away from her murderer, then fell. Dead. Twitching. A pool of glowing vomit spreading about her corpse.

Panting, the hunter took a moment to fill his lungs. Ears primed for the sounds of her brood, for any hint that another drake might follow in search of easy, exhausted prey damaged by a costly victory.

There was nothing.

No hint of grateful female. Not a whisper of mewling over wounds he'd earned in her defense.

Nothing.

The air was still.

Only his own ragged breathing echoing on the wind.

And when he turned to look, intending to lay this prize at the feet of his mate...

... she was gone.

7

She hadn't managed to run all that far from the pack, what with her short Hathorian legs and addled, heat-swamped brain. Still, Balkazar had expended a huge amount of energy in the effort to track her down. Following the sounds of a fight, thinking he'd find Sinadim's disobedient bitch being pummeled beneath the weight of a horde. Torn asunder by teeth and claws and cocks.

What he discovered instead was far, *far* worse than all that.

Lurking at the edge of the forest, he watched. Mouth agape. Chest and lungs heaving with exertion, sweat tracing the length of his back, his hairline soaked and prickling. The war chief had meant to wait only long enough to claim a piece of what was left of the girl so his prince might forgive him for her death.

Instead, he'd found a colossus.

A single infected male, mutated by the ravages of the virus, their little renegade cornered by a true titan. Larger than even Micha, a beast both long limbed and well-muscled. *Intact* in a way that made Balkazar's heart ache with seething jealousy. Over-grown, but not in a way that that left him grotesque. Not living inside a prison of festering tumors and disfigured bones—this was a prime example of glorious, Anhur beauty.

And he *was* Anhur, despite his stature being nearly twice that of any hybrid Balkazar had ever known.

The entire forest had been brightened with the fumes of potent musk. Storied and rich. A subtle, unmistakable challenge magnified by his absurd size. Nothing like the grotesque mutants Balkazar had seen so much of since his banishment, the virus had made this male into something… new.

Something terrible and wondrous.

Worthy of begrudging envy.

It was then, as his nape was dappled with a different sort of sweat, that Balkazar spotted the insidious little whore who'd ensnared his prince so fully.

Renegade.

Cringing back from the male who fought with the very breath of the Nine to spare her, she'd been made small at the edge of a battle. Insignificant. A tiny blip of pale skin and inky hair, perfumed cunt dripping with powerful pheromones that had caught yet another noble male in that sticky trap.

Derision played at the edge of Balkazar's lips, quirked against his teeth with a sneer that displayed every ounce of contempt he held for her pathetic species.

For *her.*

Fragile. Paralyzed by inaction, she could do nothing but watch as a true warrior defended his claim.

A bold statement of ownership not even Sinadim himself had a hope of competing with.

Balkazar had never skulked a day in his life, but he was doing so now. Knowing himself outmatched, enthralled by the battle unfolding before him, he hung back and watched. Concealed by shadows. Clinging to the forest's skirt as he'd never done to his own dam, eyes wide. Shocked still, for this mutant Anhur dared to clash with a fire-kin. A brooding female, no less. Standing between Sinadim's bitch and certain death, he roared in the face of a creature already mortally wounded. Every inch of him bristling with possessive rage.

Acting the guardian to a disgraced breeder.

The war chief scoffed.

Further evidence to suggest those infected with Trax were scarcely more than mindless beasts. All that strength, his monstrous size and speed, utterly wasted on a mountain of muscle that didn't know when to take and when to run, to whom strategy was nothing but a collection of meaningless syllables.

And to think such a male would risk his life for that trivial scrap of female flesh. High-quality pussy, certainly. The finest the war chief had ever tasted, but *Hathorian* pussy nevertheless.

Ridiculous.

The feral male bellowed when a blow was struck, a premature victory trumpeted too soon.

But it was one that saw Balkazar's hesitant caution shattered.

Taking advantage even as he cursed his prince for sending him on this task, the war chief skirted around the fighting duo. Head tucked, shoulders bunched, he sprinted across the barren field of pocked limestone. Ducking, his eyes flicking back in forth, searching for any hint that he'd been spotted. Marked for death by infected or predators.

The very air was held still with anticipation. Hungry eyes waiting for the fighting to end so they might scavenge a free meal.

He slipped around the backside of a rocky outcropping riddled with lava-kin tunnels. Belly scraping over stone, he went up and over, meaning to gain lofty advantage of the battlefield. He crept forward, peered over the grey edge of stone where he'd last seen Sinadim's unruly little cunt.

But before he'd spotted her, an anguished sound rent the air. The lava-kin landing a devastating strike with the swipe of a heavy, inflexible tail. The war chief was made to watch, seething with disgust as the feral Anhur fell beneath the drake's weight. Spewing volcanic spittle all over his torso.

A grisly ending for a female unworthy of such a sacrifice.

It was an unsurvivable mistake, surely.

One Balkazar would capitalize on, though it left him pained to do so. To abandon yet another male that might have been saved, who might have been added to their ranks if only they could have gotten to him soon enough. Before infection had turned him into a titan.

Dropping over the edge of the modest cliff,

Balkazar landed on silent feet at the mouth of a tunnel.

Renegade was gone.

Only her enticing scent left clinging to the spot where she'd crouched.

Mane bristling, an indignant storm rising in his chest, Balkazar took a breath and caught the scent of cum and pussy. A scent that startled, for the owner of that dried cream was unmistakable. The truth of the hours Renegade had spent outside of Sinadim's clutches made abundantly clear.

The feral had already marked her with his seed.

Balkazar shook his head, pausing only to wonder that a male like this feral Anhur would have bothered to resist a slit such as this. A breeding female, in season. That he'd clearly allowed her to run, toying with her when he should have been locked behind her pelvic bone. His knot surely just as overgrown as the rest of him.

Madness.

That sort of insanity was contagious. Rotted the mind of males born into greatness, and for *what?* A *female*, and this one not even Anhur? Who could give them disposable warriors, but not a noble bloodline?

No. He wouldn't stand idle, wouldn't bring

her back to Sinadim and watch the prince lose himself to a sloppy sheath he be made to share.

Sinadim was of royal blood.

Balkazar his war chief. Sworn to protect the Karahmet line from dangers big and insignificantly small.

Teeth bared, mane bristling, Balkazar squeezed into that darkened tunnel. Hearing nothing from the battle of giants, but his own strained breaths echoing back from the tunnel walls.

8

A t first, there was only broken branches and upturned detritus. Enough that Sinadim left the hunt to the hybrids who were trained for such things. To find only a few subtle clues the pack could follow, in hopes of bringing their feisty Omega back into the fold. Where she would be punished for her insolence. Made to atone for her daring that had been an aphrodisiac before it had become a chore.

There wasn't a need to follow their noses, though that couldn't be helped—Renegade's scent was *everywhere*. A thick, taunting blanket coating every surface the wily little bitch had touched as she fled the pack. Fled Sinadim and her duty to the Alpha who'd claimed her, and for *what?* A life skulking through the shadows cloaked in rancid fat?

For *freedom*?

Sinadim laughed.

She hadn't an honest clue what the word truly meant.

But her attempts at stealth were quickly abandoned. Her footprints growing easy to track, she'd left a trail of destruction scattered through the forest.

And yet, the wood was absent any meager hint of infected roaming where they might. Only the day prior there'd been a ravenous hoard and countless lone infected, but now, in the wake of Renegade's passing?

There was nothing but ominous silence.

A gentle breeze and the sounds of his pack searching the trail for hints of her passing. Followed by the occasional twitter of watching eyes and bottomless stomachs, but no hint of any predator. The woods lay vacant and subdued, heavy with the threat of great change, for something had gone so very wrong.

And then he saw them.

One set of footprints elegant, the other monstrous.

A hunt.

Rolling a smudge of earth between his fingers, Sinadim knelt in the spongy loam. Activating the scent captured in the dirt with heated friction.

Musk.

It saturated the ground, disguised beneath the flavor of breeding female, where moss and leaves had been crushed in a distinct impression of two bodies. Soaked into the tree bark where tiny female hands had tried to cling to some measure of safety, and failed. It permeated the wind, a scent both pungent and robust. A clear warning of a male in rut. An *Anhur* male willing to fight and die for breeding rights, as Sinadim had thought himself willing to do.

That scent promised death to any foolish enough to issue challenge.

Shocked, the prince's hackles rose up, his right cheek pulling around that gruesome scar. Stinging where his ruined eye had begun to weep because there'd been no time to tend it. No moment to sit and allow Sickle to fuss over badly healed tissue, to apply his warm compress of willow bark and peppermint, or to chastise him for clawing at it when it itched and ached.

And now it was too late, their female caught up by another. A loner whose very passing was enough to leave a desert in his wake.

A snarl burst free, rattling over Sinadim's lips. The prince seethed, his fists clenched, hackles bristling. Made a passive observer to events that had already come and gone, all but stripped of his dominance, Sinadim was held immobile by the shock of knowing what had transpired in this modest clearing.

How quickly they'd lost her.

"She did this," he snarled. "But it's cost us *everything*."

Micha placed a gentle, dark hand on the prince's shoulder, then helped him to stand. Saying nothing, the hybrid held his silence and guarded his prince's blindside.

"I would have given her first position," Sinadim hissed, inspecting the clearing with a thunderous scowl. "My chosen fucking consort. The highest any Hathorian breeder might hope to climb." He clapped the dirt from his fingers, jaw clenched around his petulant fury. The threat of enduring withdrawal yet again, topped with the ache of having something so precious only to lose it.

"She was indeed fit for a prince," Micha said, voice a dull, soothing hum.

"Alpha," one of the twins called, but Sinadim didn't bother to acknowledge which, merely focused on keeping his temper contained as a torn shirt was presented. *Her* shirt, split down the middle. The scent of this other male all over it.

Sinadim's claws dented his palms, but he said nothing. Merely set his nose to the ruined fabric and inhaled the truth. Helpless to act as another male took from his pack. Claimed his female—*their future*—for with that single breath, any measure of hope was left wasted. Ashes on the wind.

Sinadim could smell it.

She'd been tainted. Touched by the stink of infection. Even through the powerful scent of a dominant male, the prince caught the odor of corruption. And he knew, when he opened his eyes, he'd see horror...

Trax.

"She's ruined," Konjo murmured, making him jerk back from the haze of memory.

"Exposed," Keever added, the twins wearing matching glares aimed at the shirt. Irrefutable evidence of just *what* had taken Renegade from them.

A gentle breeze lifted her scent, tormenting them all with the whisper of what had almost been. The air ripe with the enticing bouquet of a female who still reeked of health, despite the looming threat of sickness. And though blackness thrashed behind his ribs, Sinadim's sack drew up, swollen with helpless want. His cock thick. Aching with the fresh memory of a fine rut that might as well have been his last.

Mane bristling, Sinadim's nape grew tight and hot.

Balkazar had been right.

"She's been exposed," he said at length. The words heavy with grit where they were forced over his lips. "Done more than simply touch an infected, and that can never be forgiven or forgotten." He let her shirt fall, watched as it caught on the tips of his claws for a moment. Lingering. "Never overlooked."

It was their one rule.

The infected were to be slaughtered if possible, but never touched. The risk of contagion too great to abide, they'd each and every one sworn a blood oath to their brothers. To the pack above all else.

To tempt contamination was to invite a swift, yet painless death.

Grant no mercy to the infected unworthy.

"Look!" The shout came from the smallest of them. Sickle, who'd wandered the perimeter of this modest clearing. Who hadn't heard the murmured conversation, hadn't given up the search for clues. Instead, he tugged at a pole jutting from the trunk of a tree.

It was a spear. Shortened to fit dainty Hathorian hands, the steel point completely swallowed by wood.

Micha whistled. "That took some doing," the hybrid said, then stepped around Sickle, nudged the Hathorian out of the way, and wrapped one overlarge fist around the butt of the spear. Wrenching it free with a grunt, he passed it to his Alpha without a moment's hesitation.

"She's unarmed," Sickle said, his ears flicked forward. Jaw tight. "We've got to hurry, before—"

"Sickle," Micha hummed, gentle. "You know what this means, brother. What happened here today." He swung meaty hands around the clearing, encompassing all they'd found. "We've no hope against the sort of beast who's done all this. To risk everything for a promising breeder."

Sickle paled, his tattoos standing out in stark relief against blanched cheeks. "*A promising breeder?*" he hissed, fists clenched. "Is that all she is to you? A warm hole capable of whelping an army of hybrid sons and sturdy daughters that will never belong to you?"

Thumb passing over the blade of the spear, Sinadim held his silence, watching the heated exchange. Lost in thought. Renegade's weapon bearing all the menace of a child's toy in his hands.

Micha growled, but didn't rise to the bait.

"We should return to the den and wait for the war chief," he said, half-turned to go. "There's nothing for us here."

"That's it?" Sickle spat. Slender, tattooed face going tight around a scowl. His cheeks pinkening, ears flat and ready for battle. "We find a torn shirt and abandon that girl to her fate, without any proof? She's *perfect*," he snapped, pointed teeth flashing at the hybrid. Standing firm. "Or have your mother's people no value unless she's being forced to milk your weak knot in payment for your loyalty to a prince who *isn't* your daddy?"

Before Micha could react, Sinadim stepped forward and pressed the short spear into Sickle's hands. "We all feel it, Sickle," he said, not unkind no matter how much the words burned. "But Renegade is lost to us."

"You don't know that," Sickle returned, knuckles white around his new weapon.

Swallowing a hard lump, Sinadim met the Hathorian's fierce glare. His scars tugging enough that his eye began to weep and itch anew as indecision warred with good sense.

"We can't just leave her like that," the Hathorian whispered, tears shimmering in his eyes. Beseeching, pain shining through the hard gleam. "To be torn a-apart. Eaten by a h-hoard. Still alive—" Choking on anguish,

Sickle's voice failed him. But the memory of the horde turning on one of their own, of seeing a lesser male ravaged by a mob of hideous infected? "It'll be days before she succumbs to the virus," Sickle rasped, tears running free down his inked and decorated cheeks. "Days of wondering if anyone will come to save her. Knowing no one ever would. And why would they?" he asked, the glimmer of pure loathing disfiguring that pleasing Hathorian face. "Who would bother to rescue her? A lowly Omega. Good for nothing, save the holes between her legs."

With an abrupt snarl, Sickle turned on his heel. Heading into the forest's gloom with a short spear slung over his shoulder and hatred fueling his soft heart.

The prince caught his arm. "Sickle—"

"No," the boy hissed, whirling. "I'm going to save her, even if that means I have to kill her myself," he added, voice cracking on a tattered sob. "She deserves that much. An easy death from someone who cares."

Wrenching his arm free, Sickle bolted. And faster than any might have expected, his slender frame disappeared into the shadows with little more than a rustle of disturbed leaves to mark his passing.

"What will you have us do?" Micha asked, his shoulders squared, glaring into the gloom.

The prince frowned. Hesitant, for he'd been trained to make difficult, unpopular decisions. Born to shoulder such burdens as deciding when a dear friend had outlived their value. Schooled in the art of seeing other living things as commodities and assets—females most of all.

Renegade shouldn't have been worth another thought, not after what she'd done. Used them. Abandoning them all without a hint of concern for the consequences. And she'd gotten just what she'd wanted, hadn't she? The freedom to make her own choices. To live beyond the rules of the Silver City, in defiance of the safety in numbers.

Was it his fault that she'd found her end so soon? That it would be gruesome and bloody, her last moments filled with unimaginable pain?

And then, in the not so far off distance, the wail of a female voice lifted in anguish—answered by the roar of a beast. One that echoed with all the way to the back of his skull, where forgotten things had been left to rot.

A wail of agony drew his eyes open. Lids dragging over eyeballs gone dry and crusty with horrified tears, his face spattered in gore, though his body was without injury. Whole.

"Sina!" High and frail, a desperate plea. "Sina, pl-please! Help—help me..."

Jolting, Sinadim staggered back from the far off sound that dared echo through decades. Eyes squeezed shut, his brow damp with cold sweat. Ears ringing with the cries of a female he couldn't help, blending with the soft, broken begging that had haunted him since adolescence. That day in the beyond, when Hadim had taken his eldest children over the wall. To see the reality of the wilds with their own eyes.

To breed a female who wasn't his wife... laughing while the world burned around him...

Mane bristling, Sinadim snarled, glaring at the wood where Sickle had gone. Where Renegade might be found. Old hatred blending with new.

Was she being bred, even now? His efforts to master her obliterated by the stink of an infected male, whose distant cries were not pleas for rescue... but for *more*...

A mewling coo drew his gaze up, to a scrap of trembling female flesh he loved so dearly. And the prince watched, helpless to fight the weight of a hoard, pain twisting in his guts as this thief of hopes and dreams pressed a blunt tip to her lips. Making her taste the thing that was to be her doom. To sip a bead of clotted cream leaking from a purple helm...

"No," Sinadim spat, hackles bristling, claws pressing into the meat of his palms.

Micha frowned. "Alpha?"

"I've no intention of losing two Hathorians in one day," Sinadim elaborated. "Besides," he said, and despite the itching scars and the long forgotten phantoms, his smile became a wicked thing. Inspired by Sickle's unwavering grit, by the seething pit of loathing burning in his gut. "Besides... Can't let Sickle have all the fun."

Cracking his neck, the prince turned from the direction in which Sickle had gone. Moving instead to face the cries of a desperate little bitch who didn't know the meaning of loyalty.

Not yet.

But she would learn...

The hybrids fell in step at his back. Micha covering his blindside, the twins on his flank. Wordless obedience, though they too wore matching grins at the prospect of bloodshed.

"Stay downwind," the prince ordered, clipped and cold. "And let's see if the Nine favor us after all, hmm?"

9

On hands and knees, Renegade crawled. Bared to the waist, her nipples peaked despite the uncomfortable warmth of tunnels heated by thermal vents. Blind, skittering through the dark, she hiccupped, trying to put as much distance between herself and the monsters slavering for a taste of her.

For a moment, after he'd stood for her against the giant lizard, she'd thought there might be more to the feral Anhur who could crush her with one hand. Thought him more than just a savage starving for her womb, that there might have been something glimmering behind the unnatural sheen of amber eyes.

Intelligence in the rotten brain of an infected feral.

And then she'd seen. The impossible, irrefutable proof that this was no lost prince waiting for rescue.

He was intact. A tail held in an arrogant arch that broadcast an uncompromising dominance—the sort she knew all too well. Stiff and inflexible, an aching reminder of what she herself had lost, it was evidence that this male was not like the others. For if he'd never been docked, then surely it followed that he'd never known the injustice of the Silver City? Never been marked as unfit for civilized life, or evicted from it.

He'd been *born* feral.

No better than a wild animal driven by base instinct.

To eat... sleep... breed...

Scrambling, she came upon a fork in the tunnel and tucked herself into a crevice. Deep as she could go. Knees to chin, naked back set flush against rough limestone. Ears flat, anxious sweat greasing her nape. And her nub— that painful memento of her stolen Hathorian identity pressed against a jagged bit of stone— sent a flare of phantom pain rocketing through her spine.

But she dared not move. Not here, where the sounds of a terrible battle echoed all around her. Coming from everywhere and nowhere all at once, she was unable to locate a source. Unable to see past the shadows swallowing her whole.

Instead, Renegade keened high at the back of her throat and hunkered in to wait.

For the next blow.

For rescue…

… for death…

She shivered, tears tracking unchecked over grimy cheeks.

Panting through parted lips, the acidity of stale reptiles left a thick, oily tang on the back of her tongue. One that saw her lips drawn back, blunt teeth flashing in helpless disgust.

But after she'd stopped, she found she couldn't move another muscle. That she was frozen. Sat pinned to detritus reeking of dried shit, sloughed skins, and what must have been a rather large larder of cached meat rotting away somewhere in the tunnels.

More than enough for *one* giant lizard, she'd found herself in what must have been a nest.

Jaw clamped shut around a high anxious squeal, Renegade submitted to the dark. Not so much as daring to blink for fear that she might be overheard, that she might be found trespassing and punished. Her flesh pulped between horrible teeth. Melted from her bones while she screamed, begging the Nine for mercy that wouldn't come.

Not here, in the beyond.

Not for a nameless Hathorian breeder, whose gods had been defeated millennia before her birth. Their names forever lost.

Muscles locked, Renegade stared into the inky gloom. Her eyeballs going dry, itching with the sulfurous fumes. Sitting so still that she could hear her spine creak with every flutter of a frenetic pulse. Straining to hear *anything*.

If only so she might see it coming.

There was no knowing how long she sat there, petrified against the stone. How long she labored for any minuscule hint how the battle had gone. If that feral Anhur was coming for her, even now... Amber eyes fixed to her in a way that no other creature had *ever* looked at her before. As if nothing else in existence held any consequence. His confidence absolute. His ownership of her body and mind a right that wouldn't be ignored.

The sound of lurking shadows made her jump, heels planted against loose shale and unspeakable filth. Ready to bolt, though it mightn't do a shred of good.

A body scraped against the tunnel walls,

one that moved in measured steps. Pausing between every step forward.

It was something big, trying to be small.

She could tell by the way the air grew heavy. Oppressive and thick. Evidenced by the subtle darkening of tunnels already painted in pitch. It prowled closer, her imagination showing her the smooth roll of hips, shoulders that remained tucked. A head that didn't move when there was prey to be had.

But it was too late to run. She was trapped. Unable to bolt, Renegade could do little but sit. Her breath stuttering to a halt, ears ringing with the whine of tiny muscles fighting to remain utterly motionless. Pulse thready and uneven as her lungs began to scream for relief she couldn't afford, but couldn't deny.

She took a breath.

A familiar scent struck her behind the sinuses, one that had her weeping relief as she lunged from her perch.

"Balkazar!" she whispered, trembling touch seeking the war chief in the gloom. Fingers traced his shoulder, the back of his neck, before winding deep into his mane. Her touch bound up at the base of his skull, she clung to a male she'd snubbed. Shameless in her need for aid. "Help me," she breathed, and crawled between his arms. Sat in the gap between is knees, where he was braced against the tunnel wall. Still.

For a moment, he did nothing but huff against her nape. Taking in deep breaths against her skin and hair, reacquainting himself with the Hathorian bouquet with which he'd grown so intimate only the night prior. Now tainted with the stink of feral seed.

"Please." She pressed her cheek against his throat. And tucking closer, ears flicked back, she stole a glance over her shoulder. Seeing nothing through the gloom. "We have to go, there's—"

Rough fingers clapped over her lips, wrenched her head to the side and away from his throat. "Shut your mouth," he snapped, and shoved her back the way he'd come. "Move."

Shivering, she obeyed. Scuffing hands and knees as she crawled, the war chief's breath hot against her lower back.

He drove her on, silent. A wall of furious muscle guiding her through the dark without a word. When they came to another fork, he tapped her left hip with the point of extended claws. Scoring delicate skin, he pushed her until the faint glimmer of evening light could be seen ahead.

Renegade exhaled, her breath a shudder of relief as the tunnel widened and they entered a dim cavern. Spacious enough to stand without a hope of touching the ceiling.

Before she could utter a word of relief, the war chief's weight landed between her shoulder blades. Pinning her flat and immobile, he mounted her in the dirt. His breath hot. Grip too tight.

"Balkazar—"

"Shut *up*!" he snarled, voice a seething grumble of hatred that went so much deeper than she'd thought possible. "You're a corruption. A vile little whore who should have been put to death before the prince caught wind of your poisonous cunt." Collaring her throat in one over-large palm, he forced her to yield as he worked at his belt. Her nipples chaffing against loose stone, breastbone made raw where she was crushed into the earth. "And now you've been exposed. *Infected.*"

It was her nature to submit. To lift the tail and appease the monster who thought to take what she couldn't defend. What she couldn't claim for herself.

One cheek mashed against the dirt, she snarled defiance. Thrashed beneath him until the scent of Hathorian blood stung her nostrils, his claws digging into her throat.

"Enough!" he hissed, going still. Adding the threat of more weight into the back of her neck. "Did he bite you?"

Ears flat, clawing at the stone with flimsy nails, Renegade hissed. Refusing to answer.

Looping his belt beneath her cheek, he cinched it tight. Made a noose of leather and pulled until her spine bowed. "I'll ask you once more," he rasped, death rattling in his tone as her hands flew to her throat. Bleeding palms slipping on the leather. "*Were you bitten?*"

She shook her head, unable to do anything else. Hip bones digging into the unforgiving tunnel floor.

"Ah," Balkazar hummed. "That's a good girl." He set his elbow to the top of her spine, the belt held taut between her neck and his fist, where he braced. Using her weight against her. And, with his free hand, reached around to cup her breasts. First one, then the other. Pausing only to tweak bruised nipples. To twist until she squirmed, the swelling length of his interest growing thick against her back. "Now," he continued, and pressed closer. "What to do with you?"

She made a helpless sound. The belt winding tighter and tighter... cutting off all hope of a precious breath that wasn't given by the war chief. An allowance.

"Wouldn't mind getting my knot milked one more time," he said, thinking aloud. "But is it worth the risk? Oh, I won't be bringing you back to the prince," he added when she coughed and squirmed, hips rolling against her lower back. Where she could feel the heated seep of wetness dripping from a cock she knew. One that had made her clench and beg for more. "You are unworthy, Hathorian. Fit to be stretched around a knot, but to carry the royal bloodlines?" he laughed. Cold and cruel. "I'll never allow it."

A weak splutter was all she could manage, her vision beginning to blur. The dim tunnel growing dark as her brain sparkled from the lack of oxygen.

She thought of Hadim, then. The prince she'd belonged to. Who liked to choke his harem females with the length of his thick prick, locking his knot behind their teeth as he chased orgasm. Unconcerned with the safety of the helpless Omegas who could do nothing but pray the Nine would deliver them into the arms of their sisters.

That they might be mourned.

Blackness descended, her fingers going lax. Slipping away from the belt as Balkazar ruminated about what he planned to do. His voice a blur of pointless syllables she could no longer distinguish from the ravenous roar of looming darkness. Heavy enough to make the earth beneath her body tremble and shake. Pounding as if the Nine themselves had been woken and raced toward her with thundering feet. Ready to claim her corpse, so she might join them in their fiery halls.

Something struck her brow.

Gravity. Punching her in the forehead as she was released without warning, unsupported by the makeshift garrote.

Ears ringing, she was allowed to suck in a choppy, ragged breath that tasted of dusty stone. The belt slack about her throat, no longer held in the war chief's unforgiving grip.

Coughing, her vision cleared. Pulse pounding in her temples, head swimming in a sea of electric confusion, she cast blurry eyes about the cave. Looking for the next attack. Cringing where she lay face-down on the cold, musty stone.

Balkazar.

His feet dangling where he kicked at the air. Choking, his face going purple, the war chief clawed at a single forearm with strength enough to hold him aloft. Carelessly, as if it were a token effort to lift an Anhur male off the ground, and *not* something to be shocked by.

A strangled sound rolled over her ravaged throat, and feral amber eyes snapped to her face.

Renegade screamed.

His mate was terrified.

Traumatized.

Those enticing black eyes bloodshot and glassy. Where she had been slathered in his scent, she now reeked of dread. The aroma of slick second to a female in need of defending.

His female.

Snarling, he shook the male who'd damaged her. The beast whose belt was, even now, wrapped about her throat. Who'd left her bleeding and scraped raw without the benefit of a taming hunt to make those wounds worthy of display.

He would suffer before he died.

A fragile, painful cough dragged his attention away from the looming bloodshed, to the place where his mate struggled back to consciousness.

The hunter spun, dragging the other male across the stone. The lava-kin burns on his skin pulling with every step, throbbing with the need to be tended. But not before he claimed his mate atop her aggressor's battered corpse.

Flailing, she tried to scramble back only to slip. Her body landing with a soft thump that nevertheless made her squeak in pain. Made his heart lurch at the thought of her fine bones broken beneath all that pale skin.

He knelt before her, the other male still thrashing where he was caught between the hunter's claws, back thumping against stone as he fought for breath. Kept out of sight of the female quivering at his feet. Discrete, so she might be soothed without being confronted.

"No!" she hissed, ears pressed flat. Lips curled back, inky eyes rimmed in white.

Adorable.

He caught the end of the belt with his free hand. Hooked it with the underside of ruined claws and used the leverage to tug her closer, despite her screeching for help. Tugging the thing loose with gentle, confident pulls that caused her more pain despite his best efforts.

When it slithered free, he snarled at what he found hidden beneath leather.

Purple, framed top and bottom by blood-red lines where her skin was broken under the surface. The growl that rattled free was a tempest. A building storm over which he had no control. It spelled catastrophe for any foolish enough to stand against him. Annihilation for the male stupid enough to invoke this storm and hope to survive.

Wide black eyes searching his face, she went white. Tinged with green as she stared up at him. A destitute creature with nothing, she looked upon him as if she saw a bastard son of the Nine. Paralyzed, unable to look away, her ears went slack. Flat, but not pinned back.

Wetness touched his knee where he knelt, prostrate before a tiny queen.

Urine.

Hathorian piss.

His mate had lost her bladder at the mere existence of his temper. Overwrought by the sight of the one male who should have brought her comfort.

Frustrated, the hunter roared, misting her in spittle. Venting the cyclone before it consumed him, he watched her eyes roll back. Watched her slender body slump where she sat, succumbing to unconsciousness once more.

But he was far from finished.

There was punishment to be dealt. An outlet to be used.

He dragged the other Anhur to his side. Set the villain's cheek and nose into that tiny, warm puddle, and ground him into the stone before wrenching his arms back. Looped the belt about his wrists, another loop sent to encircle his throat, and hogtied him so he might see how one was meant to treat a creature as precious as this. So the hunter could *show* him how to handle a Hathorian—a lesson, before he was sent to the Nine for judgment.

In pieces.

Standing, the hunter sent a savage blow rocketing into the other's ribs. A kick that echoed with the pleasing sound of cracking bone and a pained yelp that squeaked between clenched teeth.

And then, careful not to bruise his female, the hunter gathered her slack body. Held her close to his chest and folded her limbs so she might fit into the crook of his arm. Beneath his chin. Her hip notched between the hard slabs of his pectorals, he didn't waste a moment on disgust for the wetness spreading against his forearm.

He pressed his lips to her hair, and breathed her in.

Tongue darting out, he tasted what the Nine had given him. There were tears, yes. But he hummed at the salty bite of sweat honestly earned, the taming hunt run admirably *because* of the way she'd ended it. On her terms.

Turning, the hunter stooped to wrap his free hand around a narrow strip of leather, then stood. Dragging his prisoner as he stepped into the sunlight. Without so much as bothering to tear his gaze from the delicate slope of a perfect face, he lifted the other male and strode toward the wood. Seeking shelter from ravenous eyes, he left the scavengers to the firekin's carcass still smoking in the morning light.

A prize he would have dressed and stored, if he hadn't a far greater trophy to attend.

Cloaked in shadows once more, he dropped his prisoner belly-down on the forest floor. Kicking him to rouse him from his battered state, so he wouldn't miss a moment of what came next.

The hunter settled back against a boulder. Claiming a throne in the wood, his mate draped over his thighs, lashes fluttering. Eyeballs flicking back and forth.

Dreaming.

A tiny, uncomfortable smile ticked at the edge of the hunter's lips and he dragged her closer. Laving her cheek with the flat of his tongue, he pressed her essence to the roof of his mouth. Where it might linger and blend, infused with his sinuses, she would be in his every breath.

With a groan, she stirred, but it wasn't enough.

Capturing her wrist, he lapped away the blood staining her palm. First left, then right. Pausing to savor. To remember the unique mix of spices used to create such a perfect creature. A zing pulling from the back of his brain, forward. Melting down his spine and spreading lower, he saw her outlined in shimmering color. A shifting cloud that danced all around her. Thick to the point of pain, his tail bristled and stood proud. Mane shivering, standing on end, he tasted her lips next.

Her breath.

When pleasure burst behind his eyes, his throat began to twitch.

Slow at first—the muscles unused to the movement, atrophy making them weak. But when he tipped his head back, filling his lungs with a greedy breath that had gone tender with contentment, a rattle reverberated through his chest. Starting low, deep inside his diaphragm, it traveled up. A bubble of sound fluttering and rippling to life. Tripping through his throat, where it was given voice, he felt his airway spasm. Faster and faster, escalating until a deep, throbbing rumble spilled free.

Ecstasy. Pure and frenzied euphoria.

The creature in his arms squirmed, and he looked.

Hungry for more.

Ravenous.

Black, glossy pools of liquid desire met his stare. So deep, he could swim and drown without ever taking another breath.

Little fingers lifted to touch his face. Utterly enthralled by the sound vibrating the very air between them, she traced his lips before he sucked her fingers inside and sampled every millimeter of skin he might reach without swallowing her whole. Tempted to devour her flesh so she'd be with him forever, close as he could get her.

A part of him, always.

Her lips parted on a gasp, and he abandoned her fingers. Uttering that soothing, perplexing drone that bled through his chest, he lifted her. Eyes tripping over the swollen peaks of nipples made raw by abuse, he spread her thighs across his own. Made her stretch to accommodate his width, even as he scooted lower and bumped her up.

Straddling his lap, he had access to every piece of what belonged to him.

Baggy pants now taut across the tight swells of her ass, he set her core against his need for her. One massive hand locking her tightly in place, he drove narrow hips that worked without direction. Guiding her to seek her relief across his aching girth.

All while those luminous, glassy eyes never left his face. He held her entranced. Mesmerized by the throbbing sound spewing from his lips.

Enslaved to a simple vibration. A song he hadn't known to sing until she'd come to him and begged with her scent and her eyes.

Tongue rolling over the tight peaks, he sucked and soothed. Washed tender skin clean and grinned at the helpless sounds he drew from her throat. As he cleaned her wounds and saw to her, first. Wounds that drew his gaze back to the damage circling her throat.

That sound grew in pitch as his fury bled through. Laced with a growl that made her eyes flutter and roll back, she presented an enticing feast he couldn't abandon even to serve her the crumpled body of the male who had done her harm.

Claws extending, he traced the seam of badly stitched leather re-purposed to suit her diminutive size. Watched as she panted above him, hands braced against his chest, jaw slack.

Not an ounce of fight left in her, he held her freedom in thrall and found he liked the way it felt. Obsession festering behind his ribs, he drank deep of the intoxicating pleasure, instinctively knowing just what he'd done. An impulse he had no intention of fighting.

To own another so completely?

It was magnificent.

The beginnings of an addiction he would never bother to moderate.

He took another breath and forced his will into that sound, just to watch her melt. Her brows slanting up, wonder and pain blending across her brow.

A wicked grin spread over lips that quivered, and he palmed the globes of her ass. Driving his cock between them, he humped the fabric of his tattered pants and pressed his weeping dick against Hathorian heat.

Fingers searching, he sought to pinch only fabric, to pull in a demonstration of his supreme strength without breaking skin. He found the void between her cheeks and split the leather asunder as if it were nothing but paper. Exposing her genitals and pitiful tail stump to the evening breeze.

Dripping.

Positively gushing, she oozed her acceptance of her place.

As *his.*

She shuddered when he forced his rattling melody to grow in pitch. Louder, so she could hear nothing at all but his command that she open for him. Submit.

Slick wet his thighs, tacky and thick. Her scent filled the air with the evidence of her health. Lit his brain with the knowledge that screamed a possessive rage the likes of which he'd never known.

There wasn't time to taste her, his cock ready to burst.

Wasn't time to make the other male suffer for what he'd done. The hunter could scarcely stand another moment without being buried to the hilt in a cunt made just for him.

He reached between them with a hand that trembled. Eager excitement making him clumsy. With pocked claws fully extended, he freed his cock and sent that purple helm through her folds. Swiping, he sought to lubricate his girth, balls clenching at the sight of all that slippery gloss spilling at his command.

Mouth watering with the instinct to taste,

to drink her down and lose himself to the precious liquid leaking just for him.

An instinct overwhelmed by the urge to treat this tiny creature with the care she deserved. To let her adjust before he succumbed to a proper rut and drank from that river of slick. Before he tasted what he'd only heard whispered about, but had recognized in an instant.

A cry tumbled over her lips, eyes growing wider still as she felt him nudge her tiny opening at last. Both of them weary of the torment.

It would be a tight fit.

Painful for both.

Something he'd have to work to claim, to remake her to suit his needs so as not to hurt her.

Set in place, his hands found her hips. Scorched and damaged claws denting the skin as he guided her down, laid her upper body across his chest, and made her fully connect with the sound drugging her placid and demure. Keeping her tame so he might take what he needed.

His left arm bound her there—his right landed low on the shelf where hips met ass. Long fingers skimming over the tight pucker of muscle guarding her bowels, before dropping lower. To a pussy swollen with need and gushing over his length, dripping where he meant to skewer her.

A mewl kissed his collarbone.

Frantic.

A perfect match.

Claws retracting, he hummed against her throat, then set two fingers to the underside of his cock head and pushed. Testing the tight sheath fighting to reject his advance. His fingers keeping him locked in place. And, despite how he bent against her, he worked another careful thrust against her and found his mark.

The little thing squirmed, a fragile attempt to deny him. Daring to shake her head, she struggled to lift her cheek from her place on his shoulder. "Please..." she murmured, lips working against the heat pouring off his chest.

He obliged.

With two fingers, he parted her lips. Spread those soft folds and held her open, vulnerable to the invasion of too much, and just enough.

It was painful. Too tight, even without her *Biquea* glands in full flare.

Sweat beaded across his brow, his chest stuttering around a groan that broke the cadence of his wordless song. And then he abandoned the effort altogether, for he couldn't sing and take her at the same time.

Found he didn't *want* to—not this first time.

He would have her wild and untamed. Every bit the firebrand who'd earned the rights to be hunted, to make him prove his worth as her mate. And in reward, one last battle to be won or lost. One last chance for her to fight.

Using force, he pushed and felt her begin to yield. Felt her muscles tense as his influence lifted and she worked to reclaim her senses.

Trembling, hardly able to wait for her mind to return, he braced before taking that final plunge. To claim her before an audience of a bested adversary? A rival made to watch so glorious a sight?

The hunter grinned.

11

Groggy, Renegade squirmed away from the blunt, piercing pain that roused her. Ruining the lull, she was drawn from the perfect haze of that sound. One she'd never so much as heard spoken of, except in hushed whispers between nameless Omegas.

A purr.

Rumbling violence. Gravely seduction. An ancient Anhur trick to subdue a reluctant harem slave, it was a thing she could never tire of hearing—something she knew must be resisted at all cost.

Ribs compressed, she was squashed against delicious heat and yards of absurd muscle. Legs splayed, face down, she was... inspected. Prodded. Her body in a state of heated tranquility all too familiar to an Omega like her. A breeder. She knew that stretch, knew just what it was that sought to invade.

Renegade squirmed, trying to correct a bad angle. To readjust and make it easier for Hadim to take his pleasure, if only so her master would keep purring…

A huff against her cheek, the tell-tale sound of intimate exertion, and the purr died in a cruel rush. The vibration beneath her chest simply ceased to be.

"*Noooo*," she whined, now feeling the ache of thighs spread too wide. Her knees braced against prickles, an unfamiliar breeze ruffled her hair. Cooling the sweat. Bringing chill and gooseflesh.

Confusion bled through her senses in the silence, for the harem was a vault absent windows where no breeze had ever blown. Hadim not the sort to purr or cuddle. To soothe or offer comfort before tearing her apart and leaving her to stagger back to the harem without aid. Wounded and abused.

She blinked.

Blinked again.

Lashes sweeping over warm skin brushed with sparse, wiry black hair.

The harem was no longer her prison, but a terrible memory. Hadim little more than the fiend who haunted her dreams. Who'd been heinous and cruel, but was also… undeniably lazy. A male she'd been taught to fear. Trained to revere, but when she'd caused him an instant of grief? He'd hadn't so much as bothered to dirty his hands in punishing her. No, he'd been content to watch from his position of opulence.

Entertained by her suffering.

She knew that now. That he'd never deign to brave the wilds beyond the wall and hunt her down himself, which meant…

Renegade jerked. Startled and fully awake. Finding herself in a situation she knew well, but a position she'd never been afforded before. Liquid bones draped across a male chest, *she* was on top. Her ear laid atop a massive heart thundering beneath her cheek.

Naked.

Cradled.

A familiar, foreign pressure nudging between her legs, yes, but there was no ripping, searing penetration. He was poised on the cusp, a monster held still. Holding back a cock that threatened to split her wide open, but *didn't.*

And then she knew. Remembered all that had transpired since she'd abandoned her pack of fuck-drunk pack males willing to die for another taste of her.

A hunt both playful and deadly. One she couldn't afford to lose but hadn't a hope of winning.

The scent of lizards both tiny and enormous.

Balkazar's fingers crushing and cruel, claws dipped in malicious loathing wrapped tight about her throat.

And the feral Anhur with gleaming yellow eyes.

Savagery rattled against her cheek, issued from deep inside that burly chest. A growl that made her squirm in realization of just where she was. Whose claws dimpled her hips... whose purr had rendered her helpless and inert, but who had placed her in a position of reverence.

Of power.

Gathering her courage, Renegade swallowed around bruising and pain. Her windpipe crushed enough for the breath she took to whistle through the damage. Without moving her head, her eyes flicked up. Brain filled with the musky scent of heated male skin, of sweat and intense exercise, yet it was not repulsive. Not the filthy reek of body odor she'd expected from this unwashed beast, his scent was heavy. Pheromones rich and alluring.

He flexed, one burly forearm sliding over

her back before he took his dick in one hand. Abandoned his victory to taunt, he slapped it against her exposed pussy, then buried his fingers in her hair. Tangled and twisting in those wild snarls, he wrenched her head to the side and made her look into eyes that gleamed with the truth of his poor health. Made her see what the Trax had done to him.

Infected.

Unabashed, the depths of those amber eyes sparkled with a golden hue. Flecked with green. Streaked with hints of inky black.

With a grimace easy to mistake for a smile, his grip grew tighter on her hip. Claws extended, *deadly*, he kneaded her muscle and made her rock. Showing her how ready she was, that her pussy was already sopping wet with arousal. Drooling and slippery, he made her watch. Held her hair in his fist and didn't so much as blink as he worked her sodden cunt.

Heat splashed over her cheeks. She was shamed by unconscious reaction to a beast. Made to feel his ludicrous length as she was dragged over it.

But *hers* was the position of power, so she pushed up. Pulled her hair from his fist, and accepted the poise she'd earned. A cloak of elegant confidence, it was a saddle fit for a queen. Heedless of the threat of punishment, she gathered herself and set both tender palms to his shoulders. Pinning him flat against a massive slab of granite, she found an anchor across his lap. Her ears flicked back, a hiss forced through clenched teeth that grew fierce and wild. Unhinged. An explosion of vented pain and so much impotent rage, she snarled. Pressing close, glaring, she met that mesmerizing gaze without a blink.

For a moment, there was nothing but silence of a predator biding its time. His pupils blowing wide even as she felt his heart begin to race beneath her palms. Excitement an ashen sheen, his eyes grew cloudy with heat.

And then he returned her snarl with one that wasn't merely that.

It was madness.

Feral madness, hot and menacing across her brow. Sending her reeling back with the realization of what this really was.

Futility.

A hunt set and matched before she'd even abandoned that soiled den of pack males. She'd left herself exposed, still aching and tired from a night of wild, bareback rutting. Spreading herself too thin between too many. Bruised, exhausted, and worn out.

An unforgivable mistake, and one that had made her vulnerable.

Palms kneading, the feral Anhur ended her retreat with flagrant ease. Spread the globes of her ass and aimed his dick lower, sweeping through the plump petals of her slick cunt. Parting her folds with blunt heat, he rimmed her opening and sent shameful little tremors of aching pleasure through the seat of her belly.

And then, threatening without a spoken word, his knob skimmed over her asshole— making her clench as he tested that gate. Thick helm piercing a few painful millimeters into that tight ring of muscle.

"Please, Alpha!" she yelped, panicked, trying to flex her tail in submission, and succeeding only in antagonizing the beast poised to ravage her. "I can't—you're too big!"

He huffed, breath heated against her cheeks. Lips drawn thin to expose a flash of glossy white teeth.

Claws dimpled her hips in silent warning, but he relented. Swept back to where she was wet, where slick spilled over his prick, and set that searing brand of flesh against her core. A relentless press that seemed to give her the choice of where he might ruin her first.

And yet, even with her spread and helpless before him, he didn't move to fuck her. Instead, he played in the sticky river dripping from her core. Glazing his great, thick knob with slick, he sent it gliding through swollen lips. One hand bruising her hip, the other heavy between her shoulder blades, she was pinned flat once more.

Held tight to his chest as she straddled a mountain of dominance.

He began to fuck her that way, slipping and sliding without making her feel the stretch of invasion. At the height of every lazy thrust, his cock nudged at her clit, teasing that little bundle of nerves until it slid from beneath its hood.

Exposed. Eager for abuse.

Renegade gasped—spreading wider without conscious effort. Soothed by the gentle touch, by the undeniable pleasure of being handled without being harmed. By a male who would take, but one who offered her a measure of power in the act.

Caught up by a delicate touch, by the scents inflaming her fertile season all over again, she was lulled. Entranced, she reached out. Placed hesitant fingers to the hard planes of his chest, and felt him lurch—a ragged breath pulled through parted, full lips.

He snatched her fingers, only to guide them to the mess. Circled her throbbing button with the point of her index finger trapped beneath his. When her digits met the squishy head of an impossible cock brushing against her touch, he shivered. Something wicked gleaming in his eyes as he speared through molten flesh, neither penetrating her nor hurrying himself. Fucking at her pussy lips languidly. Seeming to enjoy this early stage of rut without bothering himself about rushing—as if he was waiting for something.

With a huff, she relaxed beneath him. Allowing the male to do as he pleased, she gave him every impression of submission—would have lifted her tail, had she a tail to lift.

It was expected. An Omega female in heat with a dominant male demanding her obedience? What else could she do, *but* submit to him?

"Filthy fucking *whore*." Spoken in a voice filled with loathing, that curse drew her back into herself with a snap. Enough to recognize that tone, that voice, for it dripped with the sort of malice and disgust she'd come to recognize from the war chief. *Balkazar.*

She turned to look, bewildered by the nerve. That Balkazar had the gall to intrude at the risk of his own life.

But she found him hogtied face-down, his arms held tight behind his back. Choking with a belt cinched about his throat. A captive audience to these lewd games, but still vicious when he snarled, "I'm going to enjoy watching the life fade from your eyes, you traitorous cunt. Sinadim should have sent hooks through your hamstrings and left you to be rutted in the dark—"

Swinging one mighty fist, the feral Anhur landed a savage backhand. The act of silencing the war chief all the catalyst the hunter needed to finally act.

He exploded into action. Grip tight on Renegade's hip, she wasn't given a moment to react to her spectator, to wonder if he'd been slaughtered by a single blow before the hunter seized his prick in an unforgiving fist. Sending it to test her readiness, he spread her pussy with two fingers. And with a lurid press of his hips, he stretched that intimate flesh at last.

The head popped inside, crushing the last of the swelling from her *Biquea* glands in a rush that made her breath hitch high at the back of her bruised throat.

Sweat bloomed across her nape, her forehead and upper lip. "Wait!" she whispered, half way to screaming. "Alpha, *please!*"

But it was no use. There'd be no stopping the feral Anhur who'd chased her. Who'd fought a dragon for the right to take her for his own. A male who hadn't even tasted her slick, but vibrated with obsessive want nevertheless.

Relentless, he burrowed deeper. Rearranging her guts with each inch gained. The ache of ownership one that saw her eyes roll back, even as her jaw hung slack. Watching until she couldn't. Enthralled and horrified by the obscene sight. Her pussy going from reddened to bloodless as her lips were made to widen around that girth. Accommodating the way only a Hathorian female could, the way not even an Anhur queen could manage. Not for this feral beast, so mutated by the virus.

With only a third of him sunk inside, he ground to a halt. Panting. Her powerful inner muscles screaming for relief, bearing down on the invasion she sought to prevent.

The hunter blew out a noisy breath through clenched teeth. A grimace and sweat-slicked fingers the only evidence that this moment was profound for him too. Painful, even, if the way his brow was dappled with exertion was any indication.

"He's ruined you," Balkazar hissed, still breathing. Still bold enough to speak, though indeed, his face was an alarming blend of red and purple as he was strangled slowly by the weight of his head. The bowing of his spine and the effort it took to keep his airway clear.

His cheek and brow already showing blue through the swelling of a nasty bruise. "You'll be put to death before you rot from the inside out."

Renegade's head fell back, her eyes bulging. Breath caught and held in a chest that didn't know to expand, didn't know how to make room for the thing forcing its way inside.

The hunter took that breath for her, filling his lungs before he issued a single note that rattled her brain. Purring just long enough to see her flood around him, to render her muscles lax enough that he might squeeze past and steal the rest of her.

And when he reached that final gate barring entrance to her womb, she felt him bulge against her inner wall as he bent against it. Shaking and cold. Her core melting while she shivered. Desperate—tension winding a tight band around the inside of her hips—she sobbed. Speechless and shocked.

Denied by her biology, the last of his length left outside. His knot unable to lock inside her until she was made to relax. Until her cervix drew back and accepted all that he had to give.

The rejection made him snarl, coughing up an unspoken demand that she yield. Making her gush around that hollow where she was plugged.

Renegade could only watch, trembling and impaled. The wild pace of her heart beating a tight, pulsing rhythm that begged for *more*.

Rumbling, the hunter's lips parted around a fierce grin. And for a moment, he stayed lodged where he'd fought so hard to be. Not fully inside her, but content with his progress. Humming deep in his chest, he watched her face with eyes that seemed to glow with the fires of the Nine themselves.

It was a moment that couldn't last. One that had panic rising as his hips rolled back, his cock dragging over swollen flesh that clung to his shaft and begged him to stay.

"Wait—" She hiccupped. Shaking her head, eyes wide and rimmed in white. Ears flat, for surely he couldn't withdraw without pulling her insides out?

But she didn't hiss or snarl.

She tried to follow him back.

Tried to keep that monster cock within her greedy walls that needed to be stuffed and stretched—and was *denied*.

Humming, the hunter wrapped thick arms about her ribs and popped free in a rush of fluids. Left her clasping and needy when he stood, set her on unsteady feet, and turned.

A single step took him to where the war chief lay prostrate. Face-down in the detritus, icy blue eyes watching.

Seething.

Bones going liquid, Renegade collapsed. Pussy left clenching about nothing, twitching with the threads of a built and dashed orgasm, she could do little but stare.

The hunter knelt. One massive hand winding tight in the war chief's mane, he dragged the other Anhur between spread knees. Took his girth in his right hand, then smeared a trail of slick and precum across Balkazar's cheekbones. Across his upper lip, and over his eyes, the hunter was sure to leave his mark glazed where Balkazar couldn't help but taste it.

Wiping his cock clean, he used the other male's face as a rag—then left him there in the dirt to seethe and watch.

Golden eyes gleaming, he met Renegade's aghast glare with a triumphant grin.

12

_____

Crouched in the foliage atop a granite boulder, Sickle's vantage point let him watch without discovery. His heart breaking with every moment he lingered. A lurk in the shadows, unseen. His mission one of kindness cloaked in gore. Renegade's spear clutched tight in white and sweaty fingers, and yet, he could not bring himself to really look. Couldn't bear to see what had become of the perfect, wildling female who'd run.

His target. The precious queen he'd come here to kill.

Instead, his teary glare was fixed to another. One who'd made no secret of his hatred for Sickle's kind, who'd said _terrible_ things to that tiny, defiant female while he thought no one was listening. Things meant to snuff that internal blazing fire and made Sickle glad to see him this way. A living shell wrapped around a corpse, his death all but promised.

Balkazar.

Covered in minor scrapes and wounds of a fight he'd clearly lost, the war chief had been conquered but not slain. Laid out. His own arms the lever that strangled him. Tormented. Made a mockery where he'd been discarded, face-down on the forest floor.

Despite the lewd sounds and the tear widening in his heart, Sickle's lips crinkled around a hateful smile.

Fueled by Balkazar's shame.

Not just incapacitated—Balkazar was bound. That belt placed in such a way that he was forced to strain for every single breath, back arched, his face already swollen and purple. It wasn't the accidental action of a mindless feral.

This was punishment.

And Sickle would know.

By the Nine, it was all his kind was ever meant to know.

The glint of his spear flashed in the shadows. Two paths laid bare before him, a choice to be made.

One an act of mercy for the war chief who'd made no secret of his disdain for

Sickle. The other an act of love for a female who'd betrayed him.

Both very likely to end in his death, for the juggernaut standing between them would not be taken down by the likes of *him*. Not without flawless timing and the grace of the Nine themselves.

Loyalty to pack moved him toward Balkazar, for Sickle knew the war chief wouldn't want to meet the Nine with a belt wrapped about his throat and his dick throbbing in the dirt.

But with a snarl, the beast stood, abandoning Renegade where she lay in the dirt. Giving up his back, he turned instead to Balkazar with murder in his feral glare.

Cold all the way down to his watery guts, Sickle stood. Took aim at the pretty, naked thing. At the spot just to the left of her spine, where her heart beat for another. All it would take was a single throw, and she'd be free.

She turned then, and Sickle saw anguish in the tracks of dirt marking her cheeks. In the piteous tears and ears laid flat, her knees askew, one hand pressed between her legs. The other braced in the dirt.

But it was the wide, dark eyes that caught Sickle's attention. The horror and wonder scrawled across that perfect face.

Adjusting his grip, desperate for any excuse not to do this terrible thing, Sickle followed her gaze.

Hauling Balkazar up by the roots of his matted hair, the beast offered mortal insult with a smile, then stepped away. The war chief's face left wet and shining where it wasn't blotchy with furious shame.

Utterly unaware that he was being watched. That Sickle was there to bear witness to Balkazar's greatest weakness.

Because for all his bravado, all his ceaseless hatred of Hathorians, it was Balkazar's tongue that darted out to taste what had been left to taunt.

Slick.

Hathorian slick, laced with Trax.

And with that fleeting sweep of pink flesh, Balkazar's life was forfeit. Owed to pay a life-debt to a broken oath.

"By the Nine," Sickle breathed, then tore his gaze free and dropped to his belly. Disbelieving an Anhur male like Balkazar might fall so far, so quickly. Too terrified to dare even a centimeter of action, stomach pressed flat to cold stone, Sickle prayed to gods that had never favored his people. But pray he did.

Not for Balkazar, who'd always hated him, but for salvation. For what remained of their ragged pack to band together and fight through the dark times looming ahead.

A tiny mewling voice brought Sickle's eyes up, helpless but to see the maker of that beautiful sound. The queen he'd failed, who'd left him ravaged with the choice he had to make. His heart broken by the sounds dragged from her elegant throat.

Renegade.

When he'd stumbled across a graveyard of countless dead *Volans*—their tiny jewel bodies crushed and bent—Sickle had allowed himself the foolish notion that she'd found a way to save herself. That she'd somehow used the flock of deadly lizards to distract the beast who hunted her...

That the scents laced throughout the entire wood were a storied lie.

But what he'd found was a chorus of grunted moans. Limbs tangled, tender skin stretched to accommodate a missile of flesh. Of curses and pleas to the Nine, Renegade taking everything that monster had to give. The fight long gone from her limbs.

She embraced him. Welcomed him with spread thighs and clinging fingers.

Sickle's fingers tightened around the spear, grip damp with anxious grease.

There was no denying it. Not anymore.

She was infected.

Sweat bloomed across Sickle's brow, soaking through his undershirt as he was made to watch the feral male who'd found his Renegade. Who'd murdered a perfect thing without a spark of regret.

But Sickle knew, even as his own pants grew tight and uncomfortable.

This was no simple infected animal rotting from the inside out.

Not grotesque or revolting, the horrific mutations they'd seen in the beyond were absent in this towering beast cornering willing prey. Absent except for his eyes, which gleamed with the heat of unnatural fire. Luminous and feral.

No, this creature was a force of nature made manifest. Intact, his tail held aloft in supreme arrogance, his control absolute. A true son of the Nine, every inch more dominant than Sinadim himself, a prince who'd been born to rule.

Everything Sickle would *never* be.

Something hideous writhed in Sickle's chest, then. Something hateful, helpless but to watch as Renegade went to her knees at the beast's approach. Not quite cowering, not quite submissive. Her eyes glassy as she stared up at a giant, devotion sparkling in those inky, bottomless orbs.

Rumbling low at the back of his throat, the beast stooped. Crouching to meet her limpid black gaze, he wound his fingers in tangled ropes of inky black hair and tipped her head back. Gentle as he guided her, made her look until she squirmed.

And then she reached for him. Fingers trembling when they made contact with the vast bulk of his thigh.

"*Please*," she whispered, and Sickle's heart dissolved. Burning and acidic as it slid into his gut.

Rolling to his back, Sickle clutched the spear close to his breast.

His mission altered by seething jealousy.

A new target, and this one with gleaming, feral eyes...

13

R enegade snarled around a sob. A trembling heap of pathetic conflict, she knelt at the hunter's feet. Disgraced, unable to flee or meet those gleaming amber eyes, she was left to cower while he loomed above. Trying not to press her cheek to his knee and beg until her voice spluttered and died. Until she was the thing she feared most.

An empty sleeve, just waiting to be filled.

Rendered fat over a cooking fire. Docile jelly.

He straightened, stepping around her despite the way her fingers clung, the hunter settled back against the boulder. Sliding down, he sat with that glorious tail tucked between his cheeks to protect from the loose detritus, and let his knees fall apart. Exposing a heavy sack and proud, jutting length pulsing and unspent. Throbbing against his belly. A towering example of masculine beauty Renegade hadn't a hope of ignoring in her addled state.

Not with a natural season still thick in her blood, inflamed by the scent of a male who'd fought to claim her. Who'd met and conquered every challenge with ease. Defended her. By the Nine, he'd been downright *gentle*.

All without speaking a single word, being the ruined feral he was.

The risk of infection didn't stop her *Biquea* glands from finding a second wind. The dregs of her heat sputtering to life once more, she began to produce a fresh wave of soothing, slippery slick in answer to that savage girth. Called by widening thighs, by hooded, amber eyes that issued a clear command.

That she *obey*.

"He means to take his reward," Balkazar rasped, subdued but still seething. Taunting her. "An' I'm going to enjoy watching you fall, whore. The Trax will not be kind to a pathetic, weak little bitch like you."

Keening, Renegade inched back. Teeth bared, ears flat, she retreated. Crawled through the dirt like the terrified breeder she was, lashes wet with self-loathing, for Balkazar's

opinion of her was nothing more than an ob-
servation of what he could plainly see.

A harem slave, dripping for the most dominant male. Heedless of the very real danger,
she couldn't help herself.

Renegade mewled, high at the back of her
throat.

She was no queen! Not the equal of Sam-
ina, who could bear royal bloodlines and command armies to die in her name.

She was Omega.

Exactly what Hadim had made her—
nothing more. Engineered to please. Bred to
endure.

Her chest grew tight and painful, breath
sticking in lungs that had filled with liquid
pain. Left her unable to squeeze a single plea
past the lumpy anguish clogging her airway.
She made herself small. Curling in around her
body, her eyes fell to the broad chest of the
next male to have her.

Maybe the last.

Presenting a swollen, twitching pussy not
to the feral Anhur before her, but to Balkazar.
A male bound in humiliating defeat, who
hated her enough to wrap his hands about her
throat and take a sadist's pleasure from an attempt on her miserable life.

"Can't help yourself, can you?" the war

chief sneered, his voice strained. Scarcely above a whisper. "Look at you. All slick and swollen for a brainless feral. A monster."

He was right—there was no denying the gushing, liquid heat. That she couldn't look away, even as she inched backward. It was nothing more than an instinctive retreat toward the terrible. Revisiting the familiar. Evading the enigma offering things she couldn't comprehend, she tried to return to the only treatment she'd ever really known.

"He's going to dine on your flesh as soon as you're knotted and ruined," Balkazar drawled. "Fitting end for a diseased slut."

Rumbling and low, the hunter snarled a warning and halted her retreat. Silenced the war chief with a muzzle that promised retribution.

Breath hiccupping through her chest, her gaze flicked between amber eyes that gleamed with ill health. Caught in that brilliant glare, even when a growl rattled up. Spilling over full lips.

Enthralled, Renegade was held rapt as his fist made a slow pass over his cock. From that tantalizing thick base, all the way to the flared mushroom head.

Held prisoner to his dastardly games, she could only watch, trembling. *Aching* for another taste of that delicious stretch, knowing she'd already risked too much—more than Balkazar could possibly know, for the hunter had been inside her. He'd licked her bleeding palms, and pressed his seed into her flesh. Into the scrapes and bruises she'd earned in her wild flight.

Fluids properly exchanged, she'd been exposed. Left vulnerable to infection.

"Go on," Balkazar sneered. "The prince won't have you again, might as well take what you can get."

She shook her head, hair whipping across her cheeks. The bridge of her nose. Frozen where she continued to cling to terrified disobedience, for she couldn't go to him and neither could she resist the training that demanded she obey.

Voice cracking on a sob, Renegade moaned, frozen well within striking distance of long arms. "*Nooo,*" she whispered, the ghost of her severed tail tucked tight between her knees. "Please." She hiccupped. "I can't. I *can't.*"

"Insolent little whore," Balkazar said through a laugh, strained and rough. "You dare deny your Alpha's command? He's summoned you. On your knees, slut. Crawl for your meal. Say, '*Yes, Alpha,*' and do as your told."

There was a moment of silence, then. Oppressive. Heavy enough to choke as the hunter sat there glaring. His fist still where it was wrapped around that thick staff. Scowl fixed not to Renegade, hiccupping in the dirt, but to Balkazar.

And then he abandoned his prick altogether, left it to twitch against the taut planes of a rippling abdomen and extended hooked fingers. Palm up. Fingers spreading to show the white inside that deadly fist.

Beckoning.

Something soft gleamed in golden feral eyes, something she couldn't name. A thing that hurt to look at, so she twisted back on herself. Peeking from behind lowered lashes, she curled in, where the pain was that familiar sort of ache she'd been born to carry.

Frustration saw the hunter's claws extend. Each slow millimeter exposed depicting the pocked and damaged tips of claws that had been ruined in her name. In her defense.

Tears brimmed at the edge of her lashes, her lips parted on panicked, short breaths. Ears laid flat, eyes rimmed in white.

Blowing an irate breath from his nose, the hunter chuffed. Glare narrowing as his lips parted around a noisy, rattling exhale.

But still, she remained rooted to the earth.

Unable to accept her doom no matter how much she ached for a knot. One hand darting to the molten heat beading at her core, she dared to play in the mess he had yet to taste. Conflicted. *Tormented* by need.

A low hum wobbled free of the hunter's chest. Fingers flicking at the space between them, that hum was given life. He shifted in the dirt, mane shivering, lacing a rumbling growl with a different sort of sound. And then, in a voice deep as any she'd ever heard, "Come. Let me ease your suffering."

Shocked, Renegade's head tipped, ears flicking forward. Lips parted on a soft breath.

"You ran the taming hunt well, girl. Now come." He pumped his fist, once. Hard. Enough that a bead of want glistened at his tip and his sack drew up, balls spreading on an intimate flex that made her drip. "Show me you're worthy of claiming your place at my feet."

A hoarse laugh shattered the moment. "By the Nine, he speaks! An impossible *miracle*," Balkazar said, incredulous. His words landing with all the weight of a barbed lash. "A cruel gift of the Nine, to endure the Trax and emerge intact, only to be corrupted by this vile whore. Well done, Renegade. Yet another caught up in your sticky trap. Tell me," he said, "how do you do it? Wrap them about your treacherous cunt hairs with pretty words and the promise of more?" The war chief coughed, his overt disgust bringing a wave of heated shame to prickle her skin. "Go on, then. Give your talking mutant a taste. It's sweet enough, I suppose. At least while you're still ripe."

Salty tears scalded her cheeks when they fell.

"Enough," the hunter said, and closed the distance between them. Cupped her cheek in one massive hand, and thumbed the trail of wet staining her skin. "Do not cry. The words of this creature are not worthy of your tears. Shall I make him yours?" he asked, humming low at the back of his throat. One gentle hand moving up to tangle in the ropes of wild, black hair. "A slave with no tongue to serve your every whim? Or I can make him into something new for my mate. A gift," he said as claws raked along her scalp until he found the cone of a velvety ear.

And, gentle, his fingers petted at that dainty shell until she shivered, sniffling even as she leaned into that forbidden contact. His touch bringing a fresh wave of tears that only poisoned her heart with confusion.

A golden scowl watched the tears fall. His

voice a soothing hum, despite the gruesome picture he painted with words he shouldn't possess. "Shall I make a wreath of his entrails? Serenade you with the sounds of your tormentor laid low," he asked, and pulled her up. Over his thighs where she was made to straddle a proud slab of feral meat. "Anything to please my vicious mate. To stop her tears."

"A-Alpha, *please*," Renegade stammered, both hands pressed to the heat of his chest. Trying for distance, instead she found a wicked grin and a violent embrace. Crushed to his chest, she shivered when one arm snaked over her hip.

Cheek pressed to cheek, his lips rasped at her ear. Teeth pinching, he murmured a threat with the tender care of a promise. "Shall I lay his twitching pieces at your feet? Pull bones from sockets without releasing the ligaments" —long fingers catching his girth, he set it against her opening—"just so I might breed you with the scent of justice hanging thick in the air?"

"Gods, I—" Glancing down, she was caught and held by what she saw gleaming in golden eyes. Staring down at her unmaking. "I *can't*!"

"You *will*," he retorted, and tasted her tears. Laved her cheek from jaw to hairline. "I will see my mate drink her fill of vengeance," he cooed, voice rumbling between her ribs. "This peasant kept alive for your pleasure. As long as you wish. Nothing but a stump of rotting meat, a plaything for our kits to sharpen their claws. A neutered gargoyle my mate might use to vent her rage… Anything to stop your tears."

"Please," she gasped, stretching her throat back, desperate for a sip of air not laced with the scent of rutting male. "I just… all I want—"

"Ask," he hummed, and caught a nipple between his teeth. Rolled it against the roof of his mouth.

"*Freedom*! I want freedom! Please, just let me g—"

"No," he snarled, and showed her the frayed edges of madness that infected every male Anhur—Trax or not. Possessive jealousy in all its vile glory.

Ears flicked back, Renegade returned his snarl. Thrashing against him, she set flimsy claws to his chest and tried to draw blood.

A deep rumbling laugh escaped him, then. "Such fire! You please me, mate," he continued, fisting his prick. Pumping out of sight, once, twice, before sweeping his knob through her swollen lips. "Taming you will bring purpose to my life, but you will yield to me now. Let me ease your pain."

"No!" she hissed, straining against the inevitable. "Never—"

With mane bristling, reeking of pure dominance, the hunter kissed the corner of her lips. "Submit," he murmured, and pressed her down. Made her rock against him, where he was hard and hot. Weeping for her. "Take what you earned."

And for a moment, as she smeared temptation all over his helm, he merely continued to brace. Going still beneath her. Watching as the weight of his offer began to crush. Massive chest heaving on labored breaths, unblinking, he gave her nothing to do but jiggle in a bid to take him from above. Hips caught in a cage of claws, she was held to her perch. Power vibrating between her thighs.

This was what she was.

Omega, to her core.

Pathetic by nature.

Hathorian.

But trained to endure, she'd been reborn in fire. Claimed something of herself, a tiny piece held tight to her chest. Where no other might steal it away.

"Take what you want from my body," she whispered, the embodiment of feminine lust as she tried to press against that naked heat. Slit drooling. Thighs flexing as she rocked above him. Resistance worn down to a stump of nothing. "I can't stop you. But you will never have *me*."

He moved without warning. A mountain of rippling muscle, she was dumped her on her back, an impossible weight pinned her to the dirt inches from the war chief's purple, hateful face.

"You are *mine*," he whispered, inches from her face. Cupping her face, the back of her neck, he filled every millimeter of her vision. Made her look as he bore down with a grunt. "Your body sings for me," he rumbled, and peeled her apart with that blunt tip.

And then, claiming her lips with a kiss that bruised, he unleashed unfair advantage.

He exhaled, and sent a purr deep into her lungs.

That sub-audible rattle had her eyes rolling up. Pressure rising in her head until she could feel the sound in her sinuses only for it to melt back. Trickling down her spine where it traced her every organ and pooled low in her pelvis. Heated and languorous, it was a command for her to yield.

One she could no longer disobey or deny.

Going liquid, Renegade met golden eyes.

Jaws hanging slack, she rolled her hips until she caught the head of his weeping dick where she was wet.

One curled fist braced beside her ear, the hunter bullied his way in. A relentless brand remaking her to fit his needs, she was recast in a new mold as he worked at her tight slit. Giving her no quarter until he was all the way inside, a taunting scowl pressing stolen kisses to her lips. Her collarbones and temples.

It wasn't until he was lodged against that final gate—thick base stretching her pussy to its limit even without a knot—that he relented. Purr ceasing on a final, oppressive note.

The silence made her sob as clarity returned. Helpless, but to press both hands to the heat of his chest, and do what she could to accommodate. And though her hair grew wet with the brine of her anguish, she tried to coo and enchant. Spread wider for the scourge of male flesh that stole her breath.

And then he did a thing she could never have imagined.

Hiking her left leg over his hip, his claws traced a crisp line over her skin. Touch reverent and possessive. Igniting a trail of hot coals soothed by a wave of gooseflesh, he traced her every inch until he found the stump of her tail. That badly healed bundle of nerves a constant, *painful* reminder of what Hadim had stolen.

"Alpha, *please,*" she hissed, eyes going wide. Flimsy claws dimpling his chest in a bid to distract.

Head dipping, he pressed his forehead to hers. Wrapping her in his heat, his scent. Claiming her every spare ounce of attention, his lips parted on a gift meant only for her.

"Giaus," he breathed. "You will call me Giaus."

And then he scraped his claws over her docked tail.

14

Breath frozen in his chest, incapable of absorbing the scene laid out before him, Sinadim could only stare. Jaws hanging slack. The pack hidden, waiting on his command as they watched from the shadows.

Trapped beneath pumping hips, Renegade was impaled. Her tiny Hathorian pussy stretched to accommodate a titan who shouldn't exist. A beast who'd mounted the treacherous little bitch and claimed everything Sinadim had meant to keep for himself.

But this was not the corrupted unworthy he'd expected to find.

Not riddled with repulsive deformities or rotting from the inside out, *this beast could speak.*

He had a name—a solid, Anhur name popular amongst the nomadic miners who worked the lava-fields. Those hardy few who moved from one barren sheet to the next, searching out veins of copper and other precious metals exposed from the extreme heat.

Giaus.

Muscles rippling with a sheen of effort, latticed with the marks of battles won, every impossible inch of bronzed, male skin was revealed in painstaking detail to the pack lurking in the shadows.

Chest heaving, veins distended, Giaus shifted to catch a nipple between his teeth. Working that ripe flesh until Renegade sang for him. Until his mane stood on end in a full flare of coarse, dark hair. Hips flexing where he had Renegade pinned to the dirt, possessive and greedy of the rare thing he'd found wandering without a pack.

And his tail—it was *intact.* Held stiff. Raised in an arrogant, taunting flag that sailed across the backs of his thighs.

"Glorious," Sinadim breathed despite the twisting, hateful ache of jealousy. Humbled by a beast that would stand a full head taller than even Micha—who was the largest of them— and yet was still undeniably Anhur. Sinadim could taste it on his next breath. Musk. The very wind thick with rutting pheromones. Heavy.

Pulling the flavor to the back of his sinuses, Sinadim's vision glassed over as his own rut was triggered. Swirling at the back of his brain, the addiction clawed and scratched. Hungry for another taste…

Sack drawn tight, a killing haze of testosterone and rage seeped directly into his blood. Commanding him to fight this impossible example of Anhur perfection and paint one unruly Hathorian womb with *his* seed, just so he might do it all over again.

And again.

"By the Nine," Micha whispered. "The war chief has fallen. Look."

Sinadim looked and saw horror.

Bound, made to watch, Balkazar lay close enough to taste the violent claiming. Ignored where he was trussed up in the dirt.

Blue eyes flicked up, and in an instant, their eyes met over the back of a rutting beast. Peeking between dainty floundering ankles, Balkazar saw into the gloom.

With a shake of his head, Sinadim signaled for restraint and watched Balkazar's face wiped clear of any hint of reaction.

It was little more than a few precious moments borrowed from the Nine. Time to think as his good eye flicked across the landscape, Sinadim's mind whirling for answers. Searching for the way through...

... to save who he could, and leave the rest behind.

Sinadim's face tightened, and, claws scoring the wound disfiguring his cheek, he scratched until he bled. The pain a distraction that helped to burn away the dense fog clouding his judgment.

At his command, the pack had come for vengeance. But instead of mindless, bloody violence and gore? Instead of a female they might avenge and a feral horde they could exterminate? They'd found Renegade lost, Balkazar in need of rescue. Beaten, forced to bear witness to this breeding, but still breathing. A simple belt used as a garrote.

There should have been blood, not bruises. Entrails spattered and torn, hanging free of Balkazar's belly. Twisted limbs shining white where bones poked through flesh.

Not... this.

Not a female sobbing for more, not punishment served up to a defeated rival.

By the Nine, it was *clever.*

Vindictive and selfish.

This was a male truly worthy of battle. A

true challenge for the prince who'd been born above consequences.

Cawing a gargled scream, Renegade came apart before a silent, unseen audience. A violent orgasm crashing over her, she pleaded. *Begged.* Knees widening until there was room for Giaus to pound her into the dirt.

"P-Please… *unghh*… Please…" she mewled, eyes rolling back.

But Giaus didn't relent to that primal call of pulsing, milking internal muscles that worked for his pleasure. Trying to drain and placate a male who dragged her insides out. No, he coughed up a cruel chuff and saw her orgasm redoubled. Allowing her a single breath before clapping one overlarge palm over her lips.

Silenced, Giaus cradled that exotic beauty in a fist that was meant for murder.

Renegade hadn't a choice but to breathe through her breeding, her eyes showing white. Veins in her neck distended. She could do nothing but convulse and twitch around that plundering dick, left to do little but take it.

Working her over his shaft, Giaus' tongue rasped against her nape. Licking at the bumps marking the top of her spine, even as he continued to torment the nub of her severed tail with a thumbnail. Continued to sluice through her reddened folds at ever frantic speeds.

Soaked in anxious, competitive sweat, Sinadim trembled on the edge. Fighting the urge to succumb to the rut. To charge into the fray and reclaim what belonged to him.

"Alpha?" Micha whispered, his brow heavy with concern, sloping down at the edges where that worry met his temper. Eyes tight as they watched Renegade mounted by another. And in his hands, a club. Claimed from the forest floor, he held a fallen branch with the menace of a warrior trained to defend his Alpha's horde. "I can end him. Now, while he's distracted."

Sinadim didn't bother to tear his attention free of the scene he so wished to interrupt. The answer obvious. A command already poised on his lips.

Giaus was infected.

It was plain to all who watched from the gloom, who could see the unnatural gleam flickering in amber eyes. Infected, *yes*, but this was a *new* strain. Limiting gruesome mutations to size and strength alone. Leaving him disfigured, but in ways not previously known to the Silver City. A new strain that left the brain intact.

A beast like this—blessed by the Nine in

ways Sinadim had never seen before? He couldn't be allowed to live. Every breath Giaus drew was a threat to the healthy males who'd been forced to call the wilds their home.

But to risk them all in a fight against such a titan?

Suicidal madness.

And then movement caught Sinadim's single working eye. His glare pulled up, atop the boulder where a familiar, tattooed face lurked.

Sickle.

That disobedient, infuriating Hathorian pet. His cheeks wet with tears, the soft-hearted fool.

Short spear clutched between inked fingers, poised to strike. Blind to anything but the fragile Hathorian queen sobbing beneath the male covering her.

With horrified fascination, Sinadim watched as if that moment had been suspended by the Nine themselves. Frozen in time, letting him see through the fog of rut and grasp a split second of clarity.

Sickle meant to sail through the air as if he might save Renegade from the colossus himself. As if it wasn't already too late.

As if Giaus couldn't simply slaughter the boy with a careless swipe of his claws.

Sickle would either be killed or infected.

Both Hathorians lost in a single day. Condemned, the pack would watch her abasement without acting, for the moment Giaus finally set his knot, Sickle would strike.

He knew it with more certainty than he'd ever known anything before. Could see it in the determination etched deep in that slender, tattooed scowl.

And there was *nothing* he could do to stop it.

Claws dimpling his palm, Sinadim hesitated. An absurd, unpopular thought beginning to form in the prince's mind. Considering, for it took a toll to think the words, much less give them voice.

Renegade was already lost.

Sickle only a few precious minutes behind her, a causality of his own misplaced sense of loyalty.

Utterly beyond any hope of saving, except for what they might glean from claiming vengeance in their names.

Unless…

Unless Sinadim broke free of his own petty jealousy. Shucked the rut and acted the prince.

Before him two Hathorians. A matching set. One male, the other female.

Between them?

A new strain of Trax and an Anhur stud who might be used to breed hybrids the likes of which the Silver City couldn't hope to defend against.

Grinning, Sinadim's hackles rose up.

Balkazar was right.

From Renegade's womb, an army. Hybrid titans to march on the Silver City. Illegitimate sons who would seat Sinadim on the Sultan's throne and serve him Hadim's hated skull on a spike.

Meeting Balkazar's icy blue glare once more, he signaled the war chief. Asked for a distraction, despite what it might cost.

And then a whispered command slipped over Sinadim's lips. "I want them all alive."

15

Giaus was buried inside a tight sheath. One that fluttered and clenched, those powerful Hathorian muscles beseeching him to empty himself, trying to wring him dry and leave him empty.

Pulsing with a silent demand for obedience, he hummed a tune of supreme satisfaction and obliged his precious mate. Claws working at her stump just to feel her lurch beneath him. To feel her body milking the essence straight from his knot.

He didn't stop until she screamed her throat raw, her orgasm coming hard and unexpected. The gargled wail of one whose voice box couldn't access air, he was rewarded with a flood of glossy slick that eased his path. Left her vulnerable, even as she convulsed. Those pretty black eyes rolling back until all he could see was white.

"That's it," he hummed, voice rattling with the edges of a ragged purr. "Again."

Riding the clenching waves, Giaus grinned. Pulled back and worked her tight slit at his leisure. Picking up a heavy rhythm, he pummeled her cervix with an ease denoting how *right* this was. Easing off when she mewled for more, pounding deep as he could go when she cried and begged for him to stop.

Her body a treasure that sang and danced at his every whim, she opened to him.

"Filthy *whore*," the other male spat, voice constricted by his restraints. Shouting, too loud for such close quarters, trying to make her hear. "You are unworthy of even a beast such as this. He blesses you, slut. In the only way you might ever earn—on your back. Stuffed full."

With a snarl, Giaus lashed out with the back of his fist. Redoubling his efforts to ensure those sour, hateful words were obliterated from a mind that was made to feel only what Giaus allowed.

Owning her like this? It was an aphrodisiac the likes of which Giaus had never known.

A thing he'd never give up, now that it was his.

"Please—" She choked on a sob, cheeks reddened, eyes glassy and unseeing. "Pleassee…"

Dipping low to catch the flood of tears, he laved at her cheek and drank her down. Not daring so much as a blink, he cherished what the Nine had given him. Worshiped the body he loved more dearly than his own.

It wasn't until her mewling pleas had turned into grunts of over-stimulated pleasure that he relented. Only when the cries of a female taking too much too deep echoed through the dense forest foliage did he shift his grip. Abandoning her tail stump, he cradled her bruised throat in a cage of claws and submission and made her look. His movements growing selfish and rough.

A mess was made.

Slick frothed by such vigor, mere icing on this debased cake that used to be a female Hathorian who'd dared to deny the whims of the Nine.

Her surrender sweeter than anything he'd ever known.

"That's right, slut," the other rasped, recovered already. His speech slurred, but coming fast and loud and all at once. "Take it all, show him what a prince's Omega was trained to do. Never seen any take so much so deep. But then, you are meant for this. *Only* this."

Giaus' mane rose up on a snarl, his sack growing tight as the rut flooded his veins. Tail flagging as he scrambled for purchase in the dirt, his ass flexing. Holding her hips tilted back as lips and teeth traced that sensitive spot between her jaw and shoulder. Her stuttering breath against his ear.

"Bal-Balkazar," she whined, a heartbroken plea for relief. Naming the cretin whose skin she'd soon be using as a shit rags.

Without thought, Giaus issued more of that song meant to enchant. Chest bubbling, singing for her as the insults rained down, he filled her ears with beauty meant to hypnotize. Made her gush. The very air vibrating with a mangled thing he called a purr, she was lulled into a trance as he rode her hard as she could take. Protecting her from hurt in the only way he could.

Squealing, her spine bowed until bruised nipples were pressed against his chest, she jolted beneath him. Legs shaking where they were splayed around his hips, she was spread wider. Giaus pressing deeper, forcing her acceptance of the male who'd unmade her.

"Please," she rasped, her voice strained and utterly unrecognizable.

"Giaus," he said again, just to implant himself inside her body and mind, branding her insides with thoughts of her mate, and him alone.

"Giaus, *please!*" she wailed, and came again. Gushing. Quaking and deep, it was a raw and unnatural thing.

And whether it was his name on her lips, or the scent of desperate submission wafting from her skin, Giaus knew victory when it was presented.

Hips snapping forward with a final, vicious thrust, he bellowed his triumph.

Taking everything, a powerful knot bloomed within her. One that ended her heat even as another orgasm rocketed through her slender body. She came hard enough to make him still as she clenched. Milking his knot with waves of beautiful agony as he overfilled his little Hathorian.

His Omega.

Convulsing until she fell limp beneath him, she blinked and there was nothing behind her glassy eyes. A creature of pure, unfiltered instinct he'd stretched and subdued. He watched, pleased when inky eyes rolled back until there was little but the sheen of white hidden beneath fluttering lashes.

And without a hint of awareness or recognition, she lunged for the heap of sinew bunched at his shoulder. Flimsy claws scraping at his sides, she struck with a dainty little snarl.

Teeth found their mark. Clenched and locked, she buried blunted incisors into wooden muscle and laid down a true mark.

It was a prize meant for her *Hathorian* mate. And if the rumors were true, it was one that would keep her bound to Giaus until death.

With a roar, Giaus came again.

Shuddering into the precious thing tasked with taking his seed and making life. Who'd dare to claim him, to leave a symbol of her intentions where all might see it. Heedless of the monster he'd become, she'd embraced him in the only way her kind could.

Bonded forever.

Because she knew it too. Who she'd been born to serve.

Drunk on her scent, he pawed at the plump globes of her ass and vibrated with a pleased rumble. Offered praise of such a spectacular performance he shivered as his hips pumped. Sluicing through overwrought tissue, he pulled back only as far as the place where his knot was anchored behind her pelvic bone, then surged forward once more.

He was enthralled by his mate. Totally lost in ancient, primal instinct not meant to exist between species. His blood sluggish with the rush of endorphins, rut hammering at his mind. Driving him to finally reach down and taste her slick, to succumb to the blissful intoxication only a Hathorian female might offer, and find his vigor renewed.

Instead, he found himself paused. Cherishing the moment, his every sense keyed into the small creature wrapped in his arms. Around his knot. Buried deep inside her, while she worked to do the same to him.

Giaus groaned as he bred a female worthy of his seed, his every gushing pulse dredging up another painful shiver. Another intoxicating rush that made thunder roll through his chest, taking a huffing breath of her hair. Locking her scent deep inside his brain.

His.

Awe made him shunt deeper inside her, gushing yet more of himself where she was sealed tight. His seed sure to make her bulge around a strong litter of his young if this continued much longer.

Grinning now, Giaus met Balkazar's frosty

glare, gloating. His hands dropping low. Squeezing and spreading, his fingers broke the seal held tight around his knot. Dipping inside, he coated her skin in a thick layer of their mixed fluids and bathed her in the scent of a superior, rutting male.

The air grew thick with it as another jet of seed surged up and was held inside.

Taunting.

"I'd applaud if I could," Balkazar spat. "Didn't think the little bitch could actually take that hammer, much less a knot like *that*. But then," a nasty smirk spread across split lips before his gaze slid... *up*. "Shouldn't be surprised. She *was* trained by the best..."

A shrill war cry split the air, and a moment later, something struck his back.

The impact of sharp, searing pain in his right shoulder felt a moment before Giaus came again.

Bewildered, he roared through an orgasm. Bristling as he shuddered, he moved to cover his mate more thoroughly. To shield her from the blows landing on his back. The stabbing, wrenching pain that twisted as if pulled, threatening to throw him off balance. And all the while, a symphony of chaos echoed all around him.

Screaming and snarling.

Was it the wandering infected, thinking to make a strike against him in the name of the *Primus?* Or worse, a lumbering horde he hadn't heard coming, too absorbed in his new mate?

But the slash of claws never came. Only a weight on his back that didn't belong, stuck like an autumn burr.

"You don't deserve her, you *bastard*!"

With a snarl, Giaus stood. Ignoring the dull, aching tugs at his shoulder blade—the odd sensation coming from deep within in the bone that spoke of damage done—he spun. Giving up his back to Balkazar, his female held fast and clasped tight in his hands, she was wrapped in his arms and crushed to his chest. Covered and safe, sheltered in his embrace, he set her back against the boulder and assessed his surroundings.

Knot at full bloom inside a female he dared not endanger, Giaus was stuck. Helpless to defend against attack while locked inside his precious mate.

Heart thundering inside his chest, Giaus' blood grew thick with the rut. Every pathetic, clumsy strike fueling his rage, his need to defend the creature who'd marked him. Whose teeth were, even now, buried high on his shoulder as she struggled to hold that belly full of churning cream. Her breath a sweet mist against his nape, yet unaware of the far off blows. Still drugged and sedate around his knot, he pressed deeper inside and ignored the pain wrenching at his back.

Mane standing on end, his tail stiff with warning, Giaus swallowed brutal instinct and let his knot rake against her glands until she mewled and hissed. His only aim to stop her from seeing what came next.

To distract.

Agony ripped through his skin, a sick wrenching of splintering bone and something being forcibly removed from his shoulder.

With a roar, Giaus reached. Groped blindly until he found a warm body. The bones of a skinny neck that fit nicely in his palm.

Slammed bodily against the stone, he hauled the creature over his shoulder, where it was pinned and inspected.

A boy.

Legs thrashing. Hissing. His face etched with elegant swirls and deep, blistering hatred. Dirty with tracked tears. Ears pressed flat, teeth bared, and in his fist?

A short spear dipped in Giaus' blood—one he recognized. Had *already* discarded once before.

Giaus tore the weapon free, launching it

over his shoulder with a careless flick of his wrist. Watching as the boy clawed at his forearm in a paltry attempt to ease the pressure forced against his throat.

Not a boy at all, but a Hathorian male, here to claim what Giaus had been freely given.

More deadly than he'd ever been, Giaus took a breath against his mate's scalp and bellowed his rage. Misting this new challenger with spittle. Embracing his rut and all the territorial fury that went with it, his grip tightened. Claws damaged by honest battle, extending to rip through soft flesh.

"No... Alpha, *please*... don't..."

It was a voice he couldn't ignore. A soft, feminine sound that soothed his lust for blood and vengeance, and turned his head.

His mate.

Eyes rimmed in white, lips painted an enchanting shade of red, she tugged at his wrist. Addressing him with the title she'd been made to use all her life...

... to beg for the life of another male.

"Don't." She licked her lips clean. Tasting him. Wide, dark eyes beseeching, she spoke as if dreaming. Joining the effort to save this pathetic Hathorian male from his wrath. "Don't kill him," she breathed, and touched his cheek with dainty fingers.

Her ears pitched forward in such a way that made him ache to have her all over again. To mount her once more, for if she'd had a tail, it would have been held aloft in a bold, sweeping arc. Something to match the insolent tone of a female who dared ask her mate for the life of a paramour.

The sort of daring he'd only seen in an Anhur queen, who would fight for what she wanted.

Pride bled through Giaus' brain, fogging all rational thought.

A queen. With Hathorian blood.

Truly, this creature had been sent by the Nine.

Murder forgotten, he squeezed her tight against his burly chest with one arm. Humbled that he'd proven himself worthy of such a precious treasure, no matter that he never intended to let her go. That she'd been his from the instant she'd stepped foot in the great beyond. No matter how many males she'd taken, nor how untamed.

His.

Forever.

And now none could dispute it—not even her. Not with a claim laid in plain sight, bleeding freely over his chest. A match to the wound dripping down his back.

There was a moment of silence. One lonely instant of peace where Giaus looked upon a creature that was so much more than just a tight fit, a moment of perfect happiness threatening to blossom in his chest. Centered in the throbbing ache where her mark had been set.

Something sharp and wicked slipped into the soft spot between two ribs.

A shock of pain that allowed only a gasp to cross his lips before he was sinking. Legs going liquid beneath him, hunched, Giaus went to his knees. An Omega in each hand.

A whisper skated along Giaus' nape, another male pressed far too close. Breath wetting his ear with a grin earned through deceit. "I'm going to enjoy this, you insolent cur..."

Tilting his head, Giaus looked.

Balkazar.

Free of his bonds.

And in his hands?

The end of a short spear buried between his ribs.

16

The shock of taboo raced through Sinadim's blood.

She'd marked him.

The wound small but profound, one among many. But he'd seen it before. Knew exactly what that bloody circlet buried deep in the muscle meant to a Hathorian—what it meant for the Anhur who wore it, knew just how irrevocable a gesture it really was.

Renegade had claimed this beast as her mate, in the way of her people. With blood and scars—and Giaus had allowed it to happen. Encouraged it. By the Nine, he displayed it with the unmistakable glow of pride.

And it had cost him everything.

Even if he didn't know it yet.

"Move even a muscle," Balkazar snarled, pressing the spear deeper, "and I'll tear her off your knot and break every bone in her body before I toss her into the heart of a horde. You understand me, mongrel?"

For a moment, Giaus pinned the war chief with a glare that dredged up long forgotten nightmares of the things that ate monsters.

And then, every inch a deranged feral An-hur, Giaus roared. Deep from the bottom of his massive chest, forehead thumping granite, it was an explosion of frustration and fury. One fist holding Renegade tight to his chest, the other growing dangerously close to crushing Sickle's throat.

A threat that flirted with action.

But, desperate and unable to do anything at all, Giaus' back was left exposed. Vulnerable and wounded.

The illusion of easy prey, Sinadim knew, for even wounded, this beast was no easy kill.

Driving the tip of a spear between his ribs had been enough to create a stalemate, but little else. The titan forced to his knees, and yet, Sickle's throat was still caught in a cage of claws. Choking as his face began to purple.

"Giaus!" the prince shouted, and stepped from the gloom. Intervening before Balkazar ruined everything. Before Sickle's throat was torn free of its moorings, and Renegade was ripped apart between warring males. His every ounce of focus spent on this one task, a hint of the sweetest victory teasing his senses. Fixated on Sickle, who clawed and fought for a single breath.

After all… a dead Hathorian was a useless one.

"Giaus!" Sinadim called again, his palms raised.

Wicked, gleaming amber eyes slid over Giaus' shoulder and that breathtaking, insolent glare shifted instead to the prince. Halting Sinadim in his tracks, for it showed nothing of the pain of being impaled, that Giaus feared the pack of jilted males thirsty for the taste of feral blood. Indifferent to being cornered… wounded, a handicap wrapped snug around his dick. No, the titan appeared utterly unconcerned, merely caught in a moment of weakness and waiting for the tension to peak.

For his moment to strike.

And then the prince saw the mark laid down by Hathorian teeth in a new light *not* tarnished by petty jealousy. His vision cleared of the rut and the lure of an easy victory, he saw through the eyes of a former heir to the Karahmet throne. One who'd been exiled and maimed, who knew what it was to live outside the law.

He saw leverage.

Given by a lowly Hathorian female.

In hunched shoulders and gentle hands, Sinadim found the authority of rule over a beast equal parts divine protector and merciless killer.

A male held at the end of a blade, prisoner to the knot locked fast behind a delicate pelvic bone—a seal easy enough to break... *if one held no regard for the female's health.*

It was Sinadim's turn to grin.

Hands splayed in a bid for diplomacy, the prince said, "She's a treasure, our little Renegade." He took a step closer despite the warning rumble issued from between clenched teeth. "Her bloodlines are pristine. A rare prize many would kill to claim, out here in the beyond," Sinadim continued as the pack circled. Inching ever closer... tightening the noose, their hands laden with thick branches with splintered ends. Ignoring the way Sickle's eyes bulged, Sinadim offered, "And if you let the boy go, you can keep her."

Head thrown back, Giaus coughed up a barking laugh. Mirth echoing through a voice so deep, it made Renegade quake, her slick gushing where she was sealed tight.

And then he pulled back enough to make Renegade's pussy blanch white around his knot. Tail held in an arrogant arch, his song became a possessive snarl that commanded his need.

"Giaus—*hnngh*—" A muffled squeal rolled off her tongue as he pressed back inside, nailing her to the boulder. His knot keeping her drugged and sedate. Compliant while the males decided her future.

Sickle thrashed, spittle bubbling on his bottom lip. Ears laid back, a desperate scowl mutilating the elegance of his tattoos.

And then Giaus caught her chin, mocking and cruel. "Keep her?" he asked, and tilted her face toward Sinadim with lips spread over a feral grin. "She's already mine."

"A prince commands you to yield!" Balkazar snarled. Adjusting his grip on the spear, shifting it as if he meant to saw through gristle. "Put the boy down, you insolent cur!"

But still, Giaus refused.

Seething with contempt, forehead spotted with the only hint of what must be an intense agony, Giaus' glare only narrowed. His claws prickling Sickle's throat until the skin grew dimpled and white, Renegade tucked beneath his chin.

Eyes speckled with red dots of burst blood vessels, Sickle coughed, his face swollen. Knuckles white where he tried to peel Giaus' fingers away from his throat and draw breath.

Edging closer, Sinadim pulled air in through his nose. "You're surrounded. We've won," he said, and saw the haughty disinterest. A male deep in the rut, who refused the call to do battle. Whose burly arms only tightened around the prize he'd stolen, no matter the spear or the pack. That he was outnumbered and grievously wounded.

The prince stopped, just out of reach. "In return for such a gift, I seek an alliance. That you join us, brother, and one day turn your might on the Silver City."

Falling silent, for a moment, Giaus did nothing but stare through a slitted glare. A heady indicator that the beast might be reasoned with. A deal struck. A powerful ally earned... the likes of which Hadim couldn't begin to comprehend...

Sickle's thrashing grew weaker.

And then Giaus issued a guttural chuff, the sound swallowed by a gravely laugh as he let the boy fall with a thump. Forgotten, gasping and coughing.

His glorious black tail flicked once, hips rolling back enough that Sinadim could see where Renegade's cunt had gone white around a weakening knot that wouldn't hold him prisoner much longer. Sealed by a true son of the

Nine, her eyelashes fluttered. Lips parting on a gasp that ended on a hiccup.

Taking care, his claws retracted, Giaus slipped one meaty palm between them. Circling his knot with forefinger and thumb, only to squash the last of his vigor. Working it back without breaking eye contact with the prince, all it took was a gentle tug and he was released from that perfect cage of Hathorian muscle.

"Unngh," Renegade grunted, pussy lips clinging to his shaft. Sucking and pulling as Giaus forced their uncoupling, working to compress that balloon of flesh and leave her intact. Unharmed.

Just as Sinadim knew he would.

But the prince grinned through the jealousy, the hurt, for there was a greater prize to be won. A Sultan could have his pick of bitches equal to this one renegade female.

She was nothing that couldn't be replaced a thousand times over.

Giaus' cock sprang free amid a gushing torrent of sperm, his girth in one fist, the other pressed to the earth. Seeking balance while Renegade was left to clutch at the hold he'd vacated.

Abandoned in a heap of twitching, overwrought limbs beside Sickle. Tiny hands clasped between her thighs, over her mound.

Palms cupped to catch the overflow, twitching as if wracked by persistent aftershocks from such a thorough breeding. A soft, dazed smile tracing bruised lips, she was pulled into Sickle's arms. Head lolling. Senseless.

That sight—a well-fucked Hathorian trying to plug her perfect, seeded quim—drew a quiet snarl from Sinadim's throat. His sack growing tight with the rut still thick in his own blood. The memories of his harem setting his blood alight with cravings for a taste of slick…

And the anticipation. So sweet… so close…

But the prince swallowed it down behind clenched teeth, kept his mane flat and submissive as Giaus struggled to right himself.

Heedless of the spear lodged between his ribs, the giant turned and brought Balkazar with him. Mane standing on end, though he held no fighting stance, he grinned. Gleaming, feral eyes alight with an eerie intelligence.

And then, arms spread to display an impressive wingspan, Giaus' head listed to the left, rattling breath the only indication of pain from his many injuries. "Make your offer, *prince*," he spat, and it was a command spoken in a clear voice, absent any hint of corruption.

Hand outstretched, Sinadim's lips curled around a smile. "Join us. Sire as many hybrids on the girl as she can produce, and march at my side as we take the Silver City."

Teeth flashed in the soft light. "An intriguing offer," Giaus said, mirth thick in that deep rumble. "But tell me," the giant drawled, his claws pocked with the evidence of hard battle, "what do *you* know of the wilds?"

Mane shivering as it stood on end, Sinadim stepped back when Micha's heavy palm landed on his shoulder. Urging caution. "We've survived, miner, and without succumbing to the Trax."

Head thrown back, Giaus laughed. Towering above them, one hand on his hip. The other dangling loose at his side, where the spear threatened his life. "You scrape by in a place that kneels to *me*, prince. Weak, mutilated males that couldn't hold a single tiny female. I've taken all you had," Giaus said, flicking his claws at Renegade, "and now I find myself wanting... *more*."

Sinadim swallowed. Employing his diplomacy to stop a bloodbath, he clung to the bluff as if it might stand between he and a true son of the Nine. "This isn't a negotiation."

"No." Giaus hummed, then said, "It's an ultimatum."

"And if we refuse?" Sinadim asked, claws dimpling slick palms.

Giaus shrugged. "There is no place for weakness in my kingdom. Submit or die."

At this, Balkazar snarled and moved to skewer the giant.

A strangled grunt died between Giaus' molars, but he merely reached. Stretching one long arm toward the war chief—then tossed him aside like so much trash. Pupils narrowed to specks of seething fury, Giaus stepped between the pack and the Hathorians huddled together in his shadow.

And beckoned.

Inviting the pack to do their best.

Staring into the cleansing flames of the Nine, Sinadim knew.

He'd killed them all. Tipped them outside the balance, and sacrificed the whole pack for pride.

Too stupid to abandon his bravery or his duty to the Karahmet bloodline, Balkazar lunged again. A war cry shattered the hush, Balkazar feinting and weaving.

Giaus laughed, swung one mighty fist, and sent the war chief crashing to the earth once more. Dazed, now. Blood oozing from his ears, clawing at the dirt in a bid to regain his feet.

"Kneel," Giaus said as if he hadn't been interrupted, forcing the syllable through his teeth. "Submit now, to me, and you'll be given a place of honor in the new world order. Gifts beyond your wildest imagining. A place—"

Sickle.

That disobedient, infuriating, *beloved* Hathorian pet.

Tattooed brow twisted in fury, teeth bared all the way back to his gums. Ears slicked back and held tight to his skull, Sickle ducked beneath a deadly swing, and caught the butt of the spear where it was buried between feral ribs. Throwing every ounce of his weight, Sickle roared, leveraging the threat of death to drive the spear deeper. Into vital organs.

With a grunt, Giaus' legs went out from under him. His skin blanching a waxy shade of green. Sickly beneath a sheen of dew, a son of the Nine knelt for an *Omega*... the smallest of them. All but insignificant.

And then, through his clenched and pointed teeth, Sickle hissed, "Yield."

17

F alling.

The sense of shifting through the air, both weightless and free.

Her limbs lurching all at once, Renegade's lips parted, a breath sucked through her teeth as she flailed against nothing. A scream poised to burst from chapped lips, she came awake with a hiss of pain that exploded through her elbow. An explosion of dark stars glittering behind her lids when she struck the earth.

Brain spinning, she strained to open eyes swollen shut. A crust of sweat and tears left to dry on her lashes. Her muscles tight with the ache of such vigorous activities, with dehydration.

The trauma.

She groaned, breath rattling through ravaged throat. Parched and dry, her tongue swollen and tacked to the roof of her mouth, she squirmed until her lids began to part. First the left, and then—*slower*—the right. Her vision a blur of shapes and shadows, figures doubled where they danced in a distant gloom.

She was trapped. Wrapped tight in a fur, allowed little in the way of movement.

Naked.

Her thighs still wet with the evidence of her breeding, she was on her back in the comforting dark of a den. One already thick with her own scent. Familiar. And all around her the rhythmic thump of construction. Tools striking stone, grunts of effort and the clatter of shifting rocks, the air was warm with the exertion of hard work done in a short time.

"You're awake."

It was a familiar voice, though it took a moment too long to pair with a tattooed face.

Sickle.

"Hush," the Hathorian male cooed as his fingers skated through her hair. Whispering. Blunt nails scraping against her scalp, he tried to tame her wild locks, twisting and weaving. Pulling as he worked through the tats and snarls she'd earned.

She blinked, safe on solid ground. Encased in fur, pressed to Sickle's chest, she swallowed a hard lump that stuck on its way down. Confused. Disoriented, for she *hadn't* fallen. It wasn't her head that ached from a blow. Not her elbow throbbing and raw.

"What..." She shook her head, teeth clicking shut, then reached for the memory herself. For clarity that wasn't given through the lens of male perspective.

There'd been a fight.

She remembered it in hazy flashes. Scents blending with feelings, with sounds and colors.

A shock of breathtaking agony that had splintered between ribs that weren't her own. The point of her own spear tickling organs belonging to another, despite that she'd *felt* it lancing through her guts. That she'd clutched at a wound that wasn't there, hands going to the spot where she'd expected to find spilled ropes of slippery intestines, but instead? Her throat was raw with the explosion of vented fury... *Anhur* fury.

It lingered even now, Renegade still riding the violent storm pumping through her veins when something in her chest lurched.

Her heart.

Skipping once only to freeze in place, muscles locked as a cold wash of realization flooded her mind.

A memory.

It oozed down her nape, spilled over the length of her spine and crawled into the cradle between her hips.

Pulse throbbing behind her eyes, she was frozen in Sickle's arms. Taking rapid, shallow breaths through flared nostrils.

And then, through the fog of pain and delirium, she knew.

What she'd done.

That taste… his scent, remembered for what it was.

Giaus.

Her mate.

A male who was so much more than she'd thought him to be.

He wasn't just a monster who'd terrorized her for sordid entertainment, not a beast enslaved to primal instinct. No, he was something greater than the virus that had remade him, *he had speech*. His voice rich and deep in a way that saw her clench with the memory of barked commands. Not in halting fragments or broken, one-word sentences.

Eloquent.

Giaus was a force even a Karahmet prince saw reason to fear.

They'd bantered.

Traded insults.

Negotiated.

For her.

Tongue darting out, Renegade licked dry lips and tasted sweat. The metallic aftertaste of the male whose blood still lingered on her palate... and the brine of his seed that, even now, dripped from deep inside. Wetting her thighs.

Marked.

Both of them. One inside, the other out. Mistakes had been made that could not be mended. No apologies sincere enough to undo what instinct had demanded of her. Biting him was a brainless act of submission she could scarcely recall—one that had consequences she couldn't name.

She was infected.

Already, she could feel the dull throb of fever rising behind her eyes. Pulsing with every blink. Every sideways glace.

Head spinning, Renegade tried to take a full breath and collided with a hazy wall of blistering, frigid agony. Pain so intense, she couldn't force a sound to pass over her lips until something tugged at the backside of her ribs. A bleary fog of darkness and hurt that came in incomprehensible flashes and left her reeling without a tether to time or space.

Flashes she could only assume were coming from *him*.

Giaus.

He was inside her. Every breath she took laced with anguish, felt even through the veil of lethargy swirling between them.

"Where—" She twisted, eyes flicking from one shadow to the next, seeking that unmistakable bulk of the male who was with her and not. Presently absent. "Where is—"

"Shhh," Sickle hummed, abandoning her hair to wrap his arms tight about her ribs. A hug, cheek pressed to cheek. "He can't hurt you anymore, precious girl. You're safe."

She stilled as a touch of foreboding slithered into her gut, for there was nothing safe about Giaus.

Not a single thing.

"Don't worry"—Sickle nuzzled against her collarbone from behind—"we'll figure out some way to undo it. I—I promise—"

"Undo *what*," she croaked, eyes burning. Bile splashing up the back of her throat.

"Don't be a fool," Balkazar drawled, making himself seen where he lounged in the gloom. Picking at his claws with the point of a silver blade. "You know there's no undoing what she done, boy. The beast has every inch of her, an' it's only by the grace of the Nine that the prince thought up clever some way to put 'em both to use." Balkazar stood, mane rising up as he approached, his face a mottled display of spectacular color. Bruises and split skin. "If it were up to me," he said, "we'd string her up outside camp, where we can set a trap. Use her as bait, 'cause *that* cunt is the most effective lure I've ever seen. Bet we could exterminate a good number of infected before she begins to rot." The war chief's lips spread over a knowing grin. "Unless they eat her first."

Ears flat, panic bloomed in her chest, over-riding any insidious whispers. Kicking, Renegade shucked the sweaty fur, threw off Sickle's embrace, and surged to her feet. Staggered away from Sickle and his adoration. From the war chief whose fingers she could still feel wrapped tight about her throat. Her mind flooded with horrors, choking on memories and reality. Unable to swallow both at the same time.

"Renegade, no!" Sickle cried, and caught her wrist.

Thrown off balance, she tripped. Stubbed her toe on a bit of loose rock and fell—landing hard on the stump of her severed tail with a sparkle of truly exquisite pain. Gasping, she blinked away tears, clearing her vision only to find herself staring into the depths of a deep, dark pit.

A void that seemed to breathe in time with her.

Balkazar laughed, his glare a spiteful blizzard of icy disdain. "Pathetic."

"Stop!" Sickle snarled and left her staring into the abyss. Stepping between them, palms set against the war chief's burly chest, Sickle pushed. His cheeks a heated pink she could see even in the gloom. "Hasn't she suffered enough already?"

Unaffected, Balkazar merely continued to grin, stooping closer, over Sickle's shoulder until hot breath moistened her cheeks. Saying nothing and everything, he reached toward her. Claws extending, mane bristling a warning.

But Renegade didn't give him the satisfaction. Couldn't pull her gaze away from the pit. "What's down there?" she whispered, head spinning around the sparkle of dark stars. Her muscles trembling in a lazy way that underscored just how drained her season had left her. That she'd fought for so long without rest or food.

Without water.

"Leave the girl," Sinadim said, his voice a lazy hum that demanded obedience. The self-satisfied drone of an Alpha. "There's still much to be done around camp before nightfall.

I need several dozen saplings cut and stripped, then woven into a lattice large enough to cover the pit. You can take Micha," he said to Balkazar, and inspected his claws with a critical eye.

"This is wrong," Sickle hissed, ears flicked back. "He's *infected*, Sinadim. Dangerous. He should be put to death before he escapes that pathetic prison and kills us all. But you mean to pamper him. Lavish that monster with gifts" —one trembling, tattooed finger shot out, pointing at Renegade's face—"so you can breed hybrids even more monstrous than he is. You've forgotten the blood oath you swore to this pack, *brother*."

Renegade gasped, her eyes falling into darkness once more. Horrible understanding skating along her nerves, to the spot that beat with another's heart.

Giaus. Injured in the dark.

Alone.

One-eyed scowl narrowing as the unmistakable scent of musk rose hot and heady from Sinadim's skin, the prince's mane flared a brief warning. "Are you finished?"

Shaking with fury, Sickle held his tongue.

With a sneer, the prince stood, then turned to the war chief with a casual flick of his claws. "Slaughter Giaus, then strap the girl to a breeding post and leave her in the woods."

Sickle went white beneath his ink. "What—"

"Can't have my loyalty to the pack questioned, hmm? Your demands have been heard, brother. The girl has been exposed. Or do you not recognize the meaning of the marks she laid down? Even now, his seed runs down her legs. *She's infected.*" Sinadim laughed. "And here I thought to give her mercy, a purpose that wasn't to breed for a horde, but the mighty Sickle demands justice for his queen. So mercy she shall have."

Renegade edged back, pulse hammering at the back of her throat.

"That's not..." Sickle's eyes flicked over his shoulder, rimmed in white. Ears laid out. "I didn't mean..."

The prince lunged and caught Sickle by the scruff, claws fully extended. "Question my loyalty again," he spat, "and it'll be *you* strapped to a breeding post. Understood?"

A mantle of defeat settled on Sickle's shoulders, making him slump in the prince's claws. Avoiding eye contact, his answer was a tight nod.

"Go," Sinadim snarled, and shoved Sickle toward the mouth of the cave. "Find yourself a job before I cast you out."

Renegade swallowed, hard. Enough that

the click of her bruised throat could be heard above the distant sounds of Sinadim's orders being carried out.

Only the war chief remained, scowling down at her. Burly arms crossed over his chest.

"That's it, then?" she asked, her gaze falling to her fingers. "I'm to spend the rest of my days whelping feral kits?"

Sinadim bristled. *"You shouldn't have left the den!"* he snarled, whirling on her, claws flashing. Long legs eating the space between them, he stooped, pressing closer. "You would have been protected, Renegade. *Cherished.* Given the honor of carrying my bloodline."

Renegade glanced at the war chief. Saw the sneer that curled his lips, and saw discord between brothers.

The heavy scent of rising musk drew her eye back to the prince. Made her head spin with the urge to submit.

Sinadim snorted, and said, "In time, I would have laid Hadim's severed head at your feet. A prize for the wrongs he's done to you. To *all* Hathorians."

Trembling, ears ringing and flat, she whispered, "I had to try."

A flicker of something soft shone in Sinadim's eye for an instant before it was smothered by a scowl. "You failed. And now I'm left to salvage what I can."

He took a step.

Renegade's gaze flicked back—and she saw her future in the seething dark.

Sniffling back the pitiful tears, the heat of flushed cheeks and fatigue, she pulled her knees to her chest. Scrambled to her feet, and took a step back in retreat.

And despite the languor plaguing her muscles, that she swayed as she stood there, Renegade tilted her head back and tucked her chin.

They wouldn't see her cry.

Not this time.

Her season was ended, the breeding hormones purged from her blood.

And she had the ear of the Alpha.

Time to make herself heard.

A foreign temper burned in her chest, making her ribs ache, but gave her the strength to meet Sinadim's glare with one that matched. A shimmering wave of hatred boiled at the back of her throat.

But she smiled, showing teeth.

She had no strength to fight them. No great advantage aside from her ability to whelp hybrids and fill the ranks of a feral army born in the wild. Not worthy of consideration beyond what she could be made to do. Tainted by infection that had yet to fester. And yet, Sinadim had chosen the place where she'd trapped them all. The den she'd used to satisfy her needs, where she'd left them all wanting.

It was the birthplace of a queen.

And in that, there was power.

But with the war chief arguing for her destruction? She would have to choose her words with care.

She took a breath, picking at her short, Hathorian claws as if the right combination of words might be found in ragged, dirty cuticles. "He's not a mindless brute—"

A derisive snort drew her gaze up. To the war chief, Balkazar's mane fully risen. "And you know this because you've tasted his seed and found it sweet?"

Heat bloomed in her cheeks, hurt lashing at her heart, but still. She pressed on. Defying her training, she stood strong against Hadim's son. Ignored Balkazar for the second he was, and said, "He could have torn me in half or eaten me alive. Easily."

Sinadim turned to face her, then. The prince watching her from his good eye, gruesome scars on full display. Scars that matched her own, where she was marked from armpit to elbow. Linking them through Hadim's cruelty. And arms crossed over his chest, Sinadim watched her fidget. "Even the simplest beast knows a warm cunt is better than a dead one."

"Maybe so," she said, and offered a coy smirk. "But a prison isn't built for a beast."

Chin tilted back, Sinadim's lip curled. "Know that, do you? With all your worldly, Omega wisdom?"

Renegade shrugged, her breasts jiggling with the subtle action. "It's true. I've been in a harem my whole life. Can't read or write, and I know nothing beyond the art of taking a knot without being torn apart. The only thing I really know is the Anhur," she whispered, and took a step closer to the prince. Nudity on full, spoiled display. Bold when she should have been contrite. "I know how you fuck. Know just how you fight... and I know how you think when it comes to hoarding something precious. Something to be guarded from theft. Or escape."

"Enlighten me, then," he returned, good eye glittering. Muscles held taut, yet he was unable to so much as look away.

"You dig deep under the earth," she said, and took another step in spite of the way his chest swelled on a held breath. The threat shimmering in deadly extended claws. "You call it a harem, and fill it with pretty living jewels. Lock them away in the dark and kill any who dare touch what you've claimed, but that makes it a vault, prince Sinadim. Nothing more."

Nostrils flared, Sinadim's gaze flicked over her shoulder. To the pit where Giaus was entombed in agony—and she knew power over a prince.

"Your war chief wants to see me dead," she said, and shot a coy smirk at Balkazar. Licked her lips. "Wants me strung up by my hamstrings, so I can never carry the precious Karahmet bloodlines," she cooed, that wicked smirk growing wider. "But you deny his counsel to save a beast. Your entire pack left vulnerable to infection… and for *what*?" Grinning now, Renegade began to circle. Dainty feet silent on cold stone, her eyes fixed to the prince's profile, she edged away from the pit. "Another chance at this worldly, Omega pussy?" She laughed, then, mocking herself. The bitter hurt lacing a voice roughened by abuse both wanted and not, she continued without waiting for an answer that would pick at this newfound confidence. "You offered Giaus brotherhood and progeny instead of death." Behind him now, she stopped just inside his shadow. Not touching—close enough to steal his heat. "I think you see what I do," she whispered, and traced the waistband of his pants. Not daring to touch his skin, it was a tease meant to taunt. "I think you see a gift from the Nine. One worthy of a prince, yet bound to a lowly Hathorian named 'mate' before a pack."

A low growl echoed through the cave, Balkazar making his opinion known as he watched Renegade work.

But Sinadim shivered. A full bodied tremor. "You think a lot for an Omega."

An altogether different sort of heat bloomed in her cheeks, then. One that made her heart lurch and her nipples peak—high on the flush of a point scored. "Tell me, Hadim's son," she said, low and spiked with bitter resentment. "Does it burn? Knowing that I've been given this gift before you? That I might be the only hope you've got of controlling him?"

Laughter rolled up from deep inside Sinadim's belly. Dark and menacing, but laughter all the same. "Clever little bitch, hmm?" His neck twisted as he regarded her with his good eye. Presenting a profile of male beauty that might have caught an innocent in that sticky trap, but held only intrigue for a whore. "What do you want?"

Her mind racing, Renegade swallowed. Discarding options as quickly as she stumbled across them. Knowing this one ask was a thing she might never have again. Negotiate like a queen standing amongst equals, or accept her fate at the bottom of a pit.

"I'll see that Giaus fights for you against the Silver City," she said. "But the price is my freedom. When you move to march on the Sultan, you do it without me."

Sinadim watched her from beneath a hooded gaze. Licked the edge of a soft smile and lifted his hand. Ran his claws through the snarled tips of her inky dark hair despite the danger of contamination, and said, "No."

She blinked. "What—"

The prince shrugged. "No." His smirk grew wicked and he took a step. Filling her vision with the bulk of wide shoulders. "Poor, sweet Renegade. So fierce. So... *ignorant*."

And then she saw a thing that made her flinch. Sinadim's mismatched glare glittered with the same poison she'd seen so many times before.

On his father's face.

Greed.

"It's by design, of course. Your ignorance," Sinadim said. "There's so much you don't know. About the culture you serve. The females you revere..." He stooped to meet her eye, letting her see the horrific detail of the wounds obliterating his high-bred good looks. "Your own people."

Breath coming hard, Renegade swallowed the urge to ask why. Didn't even feel the need to flee, such was her training.

"You marked him, girl. Claimed a mate."

Renegade shrugged, though she couldn't help the way her gaze was dragged into the dark. "So?"

Sinadim grinned, his mane flaring a brief warning. "Have you ever wondered why harem bitches are always bred from the back? Mounted in heat, knotted by males of a different species to whom you pose absolutely no threat? Who could tear you in half. *Easily?*"

At this, Renegade stepped back. Inching toward the exit without daring to look.

"The Anhur are the children of the Nine," he said, and stood to his full height. Arms spread wide, claws a deadly point. "Conquerors who do not bow, not even to a mate. But your people?" In one fluid motion, he closed the distance between them. Towered above her. "Servants, Renegade. In *everything.*"

"I-I don't understand—"

"No"—he clucked—"you couldn't possibly." The prince laid one large hand on her shoulder. Pulled her close and shattered her entire world. "Hathorians mate for life, Renegade. With every passing day, you will grow more devoted to the one who wears your mark. Every thought, every moment of your life a dedication to your mate. No other will ever satisfy your heat again. You can no more leave his side than fight your way free of a horde. So tell me," he snarled, and caught her beneath the armpits. Lifting her high above the ground, he spun, pressed his lips to the shell of her satin ear, and said, *"Does it burn?"*

And then she was sailing through the air, weightless and free.

Falling into darkness.

18

Setting his teeth to a hank of charred meat, Balkazar scowled into the flames. Sat alone on his own bench surrounded by hybrids unwilling to disturb him, he chewed mechanically. Swallowed and tasted nothing. Every flex of his jaw agitating another bruise, tugging on the corners where the skin had split on his cheekbone. His ears ringing a high-pitched tune, an irritating distraction when he should have been glorying in the image frozen in his mind. Indulging in reliving the memory of Renegade's exotic face mutilated by shock.

Her spectacular failure to manipulate a Karahmet *prince*.

It was a true pleasure, to see Sinadim at his best.

The prince had reeled her in, let her ramble

on and on, allowed her to insult the Karahmet bloodline without retribution. He'd let her climb so high, just so the fall was all the more cruel.

A privilege to watch.

One that should have put a smile on the war chief's face all day and into the night, but *didn't*. No, not with Sickle sulking, his back to the flames. Disrespect etched in every rigid line of his body. In tattooed hands, a bowl of cold fire char. Refusing to eat or speak, the Hathorian brat pummeled it into kohl. Ears flat, practiced actions rendered jerky and uncoordinated with a temper that simmered but couldn't boil over, 'cause the little shit didn't have the balls to confront his betters.

"Got somethin' to say, boy?" Balkazar barked, scowling through the flames.

Sickle held his silence, working instead to turn his kohl back into a solid puck, his shoulders bunched with the effort he poured into the menial task.

Balkazar sniffed, nose wrinkled. "Eh, that's what I thought." He took another tasteless bite and stripped the last of the oily flesh from the bone, before he said, "Get your dinner."

With a backward flick of pointed, velvety ears, Sickle said nothing.

Mane bristling at the unspoken challenge, Balkazar chucked his bones at the back of Sickle's head.

Snarling, Sickle stood in a rush. Threw his things into the fire with enough force that a plume of sparks leapt toward the stars, then forced a tight, "Fuck *you,* Balkazar," through clenched teeth.

Balkazar's lip curled. Sneering at his back, he went very still when Sickle marched down to the river without a backward glance.

He sniffled. Horked a gob of spit and phlegm into the flames and didn't blink. Head twisting, he tracked Sickle's movements until the boy was swallowed up by darkness.

"His temper will cool," Micha rumbled, his deep voice a soothing purr that only served to infuriate the war chief further. Eyes downcast, Micha picked at his food, the only one brave enough to offer an opinion. "He just needs some time to deal with the loss."

Balkazar stood abruptly, paused to stretch his back free of the aching kinks gnawing at his kidneys, then turned toward the river.

With the prince taking his turn monitoring the prisoners from escape, Balkazar was in charge of the camp.

The *punishments.*

Shifting onto the balls of his feet, the war

chief stalked the night. Letting his eyes adjust to the gloom, he tipped his head back and tasted the wind. Caught the scent of Hathorian male, and followed until he heard a soft splashing. Until he saw the naked curve of Sickle's back and found the slender male bathing in the river. The slender, lightly muscled limbs of a male who hadn't been born for hard, physical work. Not the form of a warrior, yet his time in the wilds had served him well. No longer soft and feminine, Sickle was lean and rangy, the skin beneath his ink glowing with health and new strength.

Balkazar blinked, the subtle action sending a streak of pain rocketing through the swollen tissue ringing his left eye. Echoed in the right, the jelly bruised in both.

Lip curled, the war chief sniffled.

"I don't want to talk to you, Balkazar," Sickle snapped, whirling toward the sound.

And just there, in his voice, a delicious quiver of fear that whet the war chief's appetite for a hunt.

Tongue darting out, Balkazar licked the edge of a twisted smile. Swiped at the sweat beading on his brow, and took a step toward the other male. "You're an insolent brat."

"And you're not my Alpha," Sickle snapped. Arms crossed over well-formed chest, his tattoos bunching with the subtle action.

Low and rough, the war chief laughed. Claws dimpling his palms. "Big words for such a little shit."

The distant reflection of flickering flames danced in Sickle's eyes, betraying how wide and luminous they'd grown. Pupils blown wide, rimmed in white. A glassy mirror that was tight around the fringe, stiff with a counterfeit bravado Balkazar knew well, for it was the same lie he'd seen too many times to count.

The wind picked up, ruffling the war chief's mane. He shivered, a drop of sweat trickling down his cheek before it too, was brushed away.

"*What*?" the Hathorian barked, too green to do anything but break.

Balkazar took a breath and tasted prey. "I've just been thinking," he drawled, and pawed at his right ear. Working the point of his claws into that narrow, waxy tunnel to stop the infernal ringing.

"Thinking? Ha!" Sickle said, hands on his hips. "Isn't that Sinadim's job?"

With a snarl, Balkazar splashed into the river. Long-legged stride eating up the ground between them, he caught the smaller male by his scruff. Shook him about as if he were an unruly kit who needed correction. But where an Anhur had a mane of expressive coarse fur, Sickle was smooth. An inarticulate mute. And instead of a mane, he caught the boy's flesh with the point of his claws. Forced him beneath the surface of the water before he hauled him up, spluttering and coughing.

Sickle cursed, going still as he was hefted from the tepid river. Nudity bouncing, his skin glistening beneath the watchful gaze of three moons. Toes brushing the rippling surface, both hands anchored on Balkazar's wrist. "What the f—"

"I've been thinking," Balkazar said again, and tossed the feeble creature back onto the shore with a casual flick of his wrist, "perhaps your usefulness has expired."

"That so?" Sickle gasped, braced on all fours. Trying to right himself, to reclaim his footing before the war chief cleared the river. Favoring his right leg in a way that denoted just how hard he'd kissed the stone. Dragging it behind him, knee stiff, he crawled.

He wasn't nearly fast enough.

Balkazar fell across his back. Pinning the boy with his weight, he took a moment to admire the marks scoring the back of his neck. To see the damage he'd delivered to such tender flesh without any effort at all, wounds that bit deep enough into the muscle that blood hadn't so much as bothered to well up around the punctures.

"Did you have something to say?" Balkazar cooed, and sniffled. Wrapping his forearm around Sickle's throat, he squeezed, shivering with the thrill of having something so dainty at his mercy. "I'm here to help. All ears."

"You gonna rape me?" Sickle spat, and flashed the point of his teeth. Scowling from the corner of his eye all the spite he could manage. Ears pressed flat, still and non-threatening where he was pinned to cold stone. "Leave me for dead?"

Humming, Balkazar let the boy feel it when his cock lurched. "You don't have to die to bleed for me…"

"Right here?" Sickle asked, squirming against the war chief's chest. "That's your brilliant plan? Where everyone can hear? Sinadim might be a bastard," Sickle snarled, "but he won't let you do this."

"Ah, so you don't know, then. What the prince has planned for you." Balkazar laughed, breathless. Heat pooling low in his groin, where he was pressed against something softer than him. "You're going to do your duty to the pack, boy. The instant Renegade shits out her first litter of monstrosities, you'll get your crack at her womb. Your precious little queen," he spat, and shook with a ripple of cruel laughter. "She'll never be yours, but maybe you'll be permitted to mate one of her offspring."

Sickle thrashed. "That's *sick*—"

"I should throw you into the pit and let you get a head start on your new duties. And really," he whispered, "you should be grateful." A growl rumbled up, vibrating against Sickle's nape, and Balkazar couldn't help but grind against the smaller male's ass. His cock lurching at the taboo thrill. Ripe and bloated with the flush of dominance over another male. "It's the ultimate rush, to breed one of those whores. They take to it so easily. Beg before they scream. And we have a matching set." Pressing closer, Balkazar felt a gush of fluid ooze from his slit, his forehead damp with a cold sheen as he mimed fucking Sickle into the stone. "The ability to breed... *more...*"

Planting his knuckles on the stone before him, Sickle snarled. "Then I guess I've got what you've always wanted, huh?" He laughed despite the way his fist clenched, the stink of fear rising up between them. "A purpose."

Something malignant plucked at Balkazar's heart, and he stilled. Shivered in the warm breeze.

"Go ahead," Sickle spat, and pushed back. Arching his spine, he ground himself against Balkazar's dick as if bracing to be mounted. "Do what you came down here to do. Find out if I take it as easily as Renegade can, but I'm going to *fucking* ruin you for it."

At this Balkazar laughed, his left hand wandering the length of Sickle's torso. Claws scoring his hip, he pressed his teeth against the fuzz of the boy's ear, and said, "Feels like I'm the one set up to do the ruining, boy."

"Oh, so you don't know then?" Sickle hissed, clawing at Balkazar's forearm. "What I know. What I saw you do when you thought no one else was watching." Voice cracking, Sickle coughed up a bark of brittle laughter that stank of terror. "I was *there,* war chief. Saw that feral piece of shit rub cum and slick on your lips, and I saw you lick yourself clean like the helpless little whore you are."

Ice flooded Balkazar's veins. A wash of cold realization that settled deep in his gut.

"I waited because I had hope," Sickle said,

"that the virus doesn't spread through fluids, but you're sweating. Sniffling and hot. You're sick, Balkazar. *Infected*, and maybe that means *you* should be the one at the bottom of that pit. But for some reason, I doubt Giaus will have much tolerance for the bastard who was so awful to his mate. And *that*," Sickle said, gaining confidence with every syllable that crossed his pointed teeth, "is what we call leverage."

For a moment, the war chief merely lay atop the other male. His erection going limp, soft and harmless against the curve of Sickle's bare cheeks. And then, "I'm going to enjoy throttling the insolence out of you."

"Except you won't," Sickle returned, low and taunting. "You need permission to kill me, because you're every bit the slave I was, aren't you? Can't make a move without Sinadim's approval, but I have worth in this feral court. A *purpose*, even if it's heinous. But you?" he chuckled, one eye sliding back to watch the war chief with a wicked gleam. "You are obsolete. Expendable, just as you've always been. In service to the Silver City or not, you're a relic who can't adapt. So get off me, you worthless sack of sewage."

Seething, his mane stiff where it stood on end, Balkazar shivered despite the heat pulsing beneath his skin. Sniffled when a drop of snot ran down his nose and was sucked into the back of his throat.

And then he shifted enough that the little Hathorian male scrambled free of his clutches. Sat back on his haunches, watching. His eyes aching in a way that might not have come from a beating, but from something far more *insidious*...

Sickle paused to snatch up his clothing. Unable to hide the tremor that ran through his limbs when he jerked his pants over slender legs. His hands clumsy in his haste.

But before he returned to the safety of pack, he paused, glanced back over his shoulder, and said, "I don't know what's happening out here, in this place where the Nine seem to manifest in the shadows. Don't know how Giaus has done the things he's done, but I do know a beast like that won't be down for long. There's change on the wind, Balkazar. We can all feel it." Sickle shrugged, then. Adjusting the collar of his jacket, he ran inked fingers through his mousy brown hair. "There's a new kingdom rising in the wild, and there's no room for relics that can't adapt."

Balkazar didn't move for a long time after that, didn't so much as watch him leave. His back to the distant flames, he sat and watched the river slide by. Head throbbing. Growing worse with every beat of his heart, until even the dancing light of the moons was enough to make every blink a painful chore.

And then, tracing swirling designs on red rock while the ache in his kidneys grew sinister, Balkazar smiled.

For Sickle was right.

Change was on the wind.

And from the ashes, Balkazar would see a new ruler rise to take the throne...

19

C onfined in a deep, dank pit with his mate, Giaus watched her pace. One leg bent at the hip to protect his ribs, the other was stretched out before him, long enough that his toes nearly touched the opposite wall. Forearm balanced on the point of his knee, his wrist left to dangle—the illusion one of restful ease. That he was unconcerned, while his other forearm was tucked between his belly and the top of his thigh. Hidden from sight, wrapped tight around his middle. Long fingers prodding the bandages dressing his wound.

Assessing the peculiar gesture. That this bizarre pack of misfits would waste their precious medical supplies on a competitor they should have killed.

Lost in thought, Giaus remained still, but for the easy slide of his eyes.

Tracking his mate's every furious movement as she stomped from one end of their dreary prison only to turn and skate back down the gentle slope to the other side.

The pit was deep.

Floor an uneven slant.

Surrounded on all sides by layers of loose shale, the walls crumbled where they dripped, hinting at the ancient riverbed that had left layer upon layer of fine sediment to harden over countless millennia. A river that might have been magnificent, once, but had since dwindled until all that was left was the gentle creek bubbling outside. Quiet and unassuming. Rich in minerals, stained red, it left their prison damp. Dripping and moist. The groundwater filtering through the many fine layers of soft stone. Beneath them, a floor of granite bedrock, slippery with ancient algae that needed no light to grow.

It was a miserable place to heal. Rife with potential for his wounds to fester, but Giaus made no effort to escape. Not while his every breath was laced with hurt, not with his precious mate already sniffling with the onset of fever. Even through the gloom, he saw the way her brows bunched, eyes squeezed shut as she tried not to whine. The sour stench oozing from her pores stuck to the back of his sinuses, obliterating the heady scent of a breeding, healthy female with one that was quickly becoming ill.

Restless.

Pacing, pacing, *pacing*.

He followed her progress with an obsessive vigilance. Watched her feet skip and stumble over the sloped floor, her fingers clinging to the jagged walls.

Monitoring her for the signs of descent he knew so well, so he might be ready for her inevitable fall.

All the while, admiring the rounded cheeks of a tight ass bruised with his fingerprints, scored by the tips of his claws. His eyes fixed to the flex of muscle. A thick, full bottom that was achingly absent the flick of her tail. He mapped the exquisite curve of thighs that met and blended with a trim waist. Scrutinized where her spine was etched with the markings of her treasured lineage. A harem Omega, born to breed for a prince. She was meant only to submit and be dependent on the charity of her master, and yet, here she stood. Absent the poke of bones through skin that spoke of a female willing to do anything for a meager bite of food.

A true marvel, his mate. One made just for him. Given by the Nine themselves, for how else might she have wandered the wilds without the journey showing on her delicate skin? In this place that bowed to *him*. Where he'd carved out a territory even the hordes of doomed infected dared not breech.

But he had none of that now.

He'd abandoned his dominion…

… to claim *her*.

His Renegade Omega.

It was a name that suited her odd temperament. Rebellious and fierce, despite her low-born nature.

Hissing, ears laid flat, she turned and paced toward him once more. Her feet careful on the slippery slope of their intimate den.

Giaus' amber gaze dropped to her nipples. Caught on the bounce and jiggle of fatty, ripe flesh. Held utterly still despite how he wanted to touch, he waited. Anticipating the perfect moment to strike, for her pacing to falter when his little warrior finally burned herself out. Hungry for the looming tantrum to boil over, so he might soothe her temper then knot her pliant. Let her drink down as much of his seed as she could swallow so she might sleep well in his arms after so vigorous a claiming.

Her belly full of him.

Luminous dark eyes flicked toward his face, then skittered away. His female nervous to be in his presence. Trying to deny the comfort he offered—that she so *desperately* needed—she scoffed and twisted away. Hiding her nudity from inspection.

Rumbling, Giaus' lips twitched, but that was all.

Even now, after he'd won her most precious gift, he wanted another taste. Her defiance an aphrodisiac that saw his sack swell with another loaded dose meant to tame her. The muscles in his throat itching to sing for her. To soothe her wildling spirit and make her see the beast she'd claimed for what he really was.

But he didn't move.

Merely settled in to wait her out. Back pressed to a wall of uneven, loose shale, tracing the bandage with the point of his claw.

The wound had been packed, stank faintly of sweet herbs. Ached only when he prodded the edges in a way that suggested there was some sort of numbing herb added in the poultice.

It started with a sniffle.

Reddened nose and cheeks, drooping ears and glassy eyes. Shivering uncontrollably in the damp chill of their prison, Renegade's hand dropped to her side. Rubbing as if in pain, she ended her furious pacing at last, twisted and sent a glare over her shoulder. Scowling at the bandage wrapped about his ribs, she said, "Stop it."

And for a moment, he simply continued to watch her. Trying to recall what he knew of her kind, of the Hathorian mating bond and all its many curious attributes the stuff of legend. Privileged knowledge meant only for the most elite Anhur with the largest harems.

Certainly not for the likes of *him.*

Until she'd laid her claim in blood and treasured scars.

Lips spreading over a taunting grin, Giaus tilted his chin toward her.

And then, hidden from her narrowed gaze, he dug one finger into his wound.

She sucked a breath between her teeth, pupils tiny pricks of seething black. Fists clenched at her sides, she turned to face him. Forgetting her nudity, ears pinned flat, she bared the smooth line of her teeth. "I said, *leave it alone.*"

Giaus shrugged, and said nothing.

Knowing just how it would rankle his vicious mate. That she'd just confirmed at least one of the myths of the mating bond.

She could feel him.

Grinning, his point made, Giaus abandoned his wound. His blood swamped with arousal at the sheer weight of possibility. Having a female who might anticipate his every need? One naturally submissive, already conditioned to obey.

His.

Completely.

Renegade stumbled back, teeth gleaming white in the gloom. "I don't want this. Don't want *you.*"

At this, Giaus' chest rumbled with mirth, his ribs issuing a creaking protest. His unnatural golden gaze fixed to her face, memorizing every inch of this glorious creature before he bothered himself to move. Dropping one shoulder, he let her see the lie she tried to sell. The imprint of her teeth left high on the muscle of his shoulder.

"That means *nothing*," she snarled, but he saw the way she shivered. Wobbling on legs she couldn't quite seem to control. "I'll find a way to break this infernal bond."

"I hope you do," he said at last, and resumed his watchful vigilance of so resourceful and indomitable a spirit. "That you run as fast and as far as you can." He licked his lips. "But the next hunt will not be so gentle."

For a moment, Renegade chewed at her

lip. Sniffling as she stared him down, her eyes rimmed in red, over-bright and sunken. And then she lost her footing, slipped and caught herself before her knees buckled, and said, "You're just like the rest of them, Giaus. I don't need to see the way you look at me to know you think me a sleeve for your cock"— she scrubbed at her breastbone, ears laid out, tears sparkling on her lashes—"I can *feel* it! Right here." She hiccupped, a tiny sound that struck him with the weight of a feral horde, before she pressed her eyes into the crook of her elbow to banish those tears. "And it hurts…"

"Omega," Giaus hummed, rattling and broken. He extended his left arm, palm up. An offer of comfort despite his confusion at her words, her actions. That his mate felt his pain was a passing concern that would fade by the hour, but her rejection? It rankled and burned. Wormed deep inside his chest and evoked a thing he'd never known before. An obstacle he couldn't easily overcome. "It's the killing fever," he rumbled at length, voice laced with the barest whisper of a drugging purr. Seeking to force her compliance when she swayed again, squinting at him with unfocused, bleary eyes. "Come. Sleep now, through the worst of it. When you wake, it will be with new eyes."

But through chattering teeth, she sneered and resumed her fretting. Turned her back so he couldn't see those tight little nipples that begged for the tranquil roll of his tongue.

She wanted a fight.

So a fight she would have.

"Shall I mount you as we quarrel?" he drawled, and let his offer of comfort slap to the slimy granite. Frustrated, his fist curled to hide the point of extended claws. "Shall I take you now, while your temper is hot? Is that what you need to end this nonsense? A knot to keep you placid?"

"You don't own me!" she snarled, vibrating all over. Incensed.

Completely adorable, from flattened ears to her elegant battle stance. As if she meant to rail against him.

As if she had even half a chance.

Fighting back the amusement, he said, "You reject what you do not understand."

She shook her head. Tears spilling over her lashes, despite the helpless step she took toward him. "I reject a new master who sees only a womb!" she cried, and sniffled. Flushed with shame as she trembled before him, a fine layer of dew gathering on her brow. "One who can't see... *me*."

So Giaus looked and saw high, elegant

cheekbones. A creature of his most wild musings brought to life, who denied him at every turn, whose scent alone was enough to send him into a mindless, all-consuming rut. Enough to put him off food and drink, abandon all that he'd built to the roaming hordes of hopeless lost. Enough to see him challenge an entire pack for the rights to claim a single precious, high-bred female who took in every monstrous inch of him and begged for more.

"What—" She staggered back, thumping against the wall. Filling their small space with the stink of terror, hands pressed to her breastbone once more. "What is this?"

Shameless, Giaus took advantage, for that was the curse of the Omega. That she'd feel what she did to him. "Let me soothe you, mate," he rumbled, watching her melt. Her pupils ballooning out, to swallow the dark outer ring of those beloved dark eyes.

Teeth flashing, Renegade persisted. Knees trembling, chewing at her lip.

And so he was the first to bend. Purring a symphony for the fierce little thing who *needed* the comfort only he might offer, Giaus reached and pulled her close. Cupped one hip in a massive hand meant for murder, he squeezed something delicate, and said, "This will pass."

"Please—" Renegade stumbled, taking the final step toward him before giving up. Before her knees turned to liquid, and she was caught up. "Just... just let me go..."

Giaus hummed as he swept her off her feet, and said simply, "No," as he cradled her in the crook of one massive arm. Crooning for the beautiful, damaged thing just so he could watch her eyelids grow heavy. The stabbing pain in his ribs forgotten.

"Giaus..." she slurred, her ears tipping forward as he shifted. Set her high on his belly, and left her sprawled across his chest.

"Sleep," he said, and planted one large palm over her bellybutton. Kneading the spot where his seed would flourish, that delicate cradle that could ignite war between the Anhur. "The Trax will take the place of all this weakness and frailty. You'll wake stronger, Renegade. My vicious warrior."

She keened, one last defiance before she obeyed. A broken whimper pressed into the scalding heat of his chest. And then, "I... I was trained to be a whore... I can't be... *this*..."

He adjusted the swollen length of his prick and pressed a kiss to the crown of her head.

"You can," he rattled, redoubling the weight of his purr as he settled her liquid body over his lap. Feet tucked in the bend of his opposite elbow, cautious of his wounds—willing to suffer anything for this one tiny female. "Prove yourself worthy of the name you bear." He traced the length of her spine with a single extended claw, making her shiver in his arms. "Be a Renegade, and as a reward, I shall have these etchings struck from your skin."

"How?" She yawned, pressed her nose to the spot that bore her mark. Breath feathering against the underside of his chin as she succumbed. "We're... in a prison..." she murmured, and went limp in his arms.

Giaus purred for his mate until the fight left her, and so she didn't hear him when he said, "Perhaps, but not for long..."

20

Staggering, fingers pressed to the jagged marks left by Balkazar's claws, Sickle clung to the shadows. His knee throbbing only half so viciously as his hip, where he'd hit the stone hard enough to bruise the bone. Every step a fight he couldn't lose, one stride closer to tending his wounds.

Skirting the welcoming warmth of fire ringed by hybrids who hadn't come to his aid, he did little more than glance in their direction. Keever, Konjo and Micha—all huddled together, side-by-side-by-side, their backs to the river. Shoulders hunched.

Sickle's lips curled around a sneer, though the gesture held no real heat. Not for males who'd been bound together by circumstance, who knew what it was to scrape for survival.

To look the other way and preserve self above pack.

Blood oozed from the deepest of the wounds, making his fingers slip in the gore. Sickle hissed, readjusted his grip to encourage the bleeding despite the shiver it sent through his blood. Hoping the wound might flush itself of whatever horror was beneath Balkazar's claws.

That it wasn't already too late.

Ears flicking back and forth, scanning the simmering dark for any whisper of looming attack, Sickle braced for the next violation in a way not even female Hathorians could empathize with.

Not really, for they were kept safe —*guarded*—deep inside their harems. Raised on sisterhood, used only for a few nights while in season before they were left to the comforting dark. Ignored as one might disregard a table laden with delicate, breakable finery until the occasion warranted their use.

But his kind?

Hathorian males?

He'd been a pet.

Raised in the courts. Traded amongst warring queens, he'd learned too young that the aggression of Anhur was above gender or status. That he was nothing, had *nothing* but his wits and the scraps of information he managed to steal.

But his choices had never been his own. What to wear, who to serve, right down to the changes made to the flesh on his body. Subject to the whims of a predatory species that cooed over him just as readily as they swung a merciless backhand.

Even his banishment, the loss of his tail, *all of it* had been a means of punishment for another. His presence in this pack meant to torment the prince through his withdrawal from the rut—from the near constant breeding of his harem Omegas. Sinadim's addiction to Hathorian slick that had left him in agony when he'd been made to go without.

An agony the prince's father had meant Sickle to endure, despite his lack of lubricating glands and that he was missing one key hole.

And yet, despite being raised on a diet rich in cruelty—and that any other high-born male would have succumbed to the temptation without much prompting—Sinadim had never once looked at Sickle in a way that made his tail stub flex in terrified submission.

Until now.

If everything Balkazar had said was true, if he was destined to be nothing more than a source of Hathorian seed, it wouldn't be long before Sickle's other duties to the pack were called into question.

Wouldn't be long before the Anhur found him... a *new* position.

One that suited a breeder...

On his knees... bent over the dinner table... a fist in his hair and a knot sealing him from both ends.

It wasn't the first time he'd fallen beneath the snapping hips of Anhur males.

But it would be the last.

Limping toward the yawning mouth of the cave, Sickle hobbled past the steaming drop pools. Skirted the heap of soiled clothing that was all that remained of Renegade's nest, and entered her den.

Ears twitching at every tiny sound, he scanned the gloom for any sign that the Alpha had noticed his entrance. Moving on the balls of his feet, silent in the way he'd been born to be, his breath intentionally held so he might keep his head clear of the scent of slick... of any hint of what might be happening where he couldn't see it. His attention divided, Sickle knelt and hooked his fingers beneath the strap of a tidy leather pack.

His medical supplies.

Before the Alpha might even notice he'd

come, Sickle was gone. Moving not to the lie of protection with his brothers, he veered left and found a ledge. A few crumbling handholds and a footing wide enough for him to haul himself off the ground. Spidering up, he climbed hand over fist. The muscles beneath his ink twisting and bunching as he scrambled up. Still favoring the hurt in his knee and hip, using that leg as little as he could, he climbed until the ledge grew wide enough to bear his weight.

An outcropping too slim and fragile for any of the Anhur to follow, he turned and worked with his back pressed to the sheer face of red stone. Pack slung over his shoulder, he inched along until he claimed an outcropping not visible from the clearing below.

Trembling and in pain, soaked in a cold sweat, he sat. Let his head fall back where it thumped against the cliff face.

It was quiet.

Peaceful in a way Sickle had never known before, almost… uncomfortable in the hush. A thing he didn't know and couldn't name. But for the first time in working memory, he took a breath that wasn't saturated with the stink of Anhur pheromones. The scent of smoke a teasing hint where it was thinned by the breeze.

This was a place to think without being made to choke on the tensions rising between Anhur. On the horrors Balkazar had whispered in the dark. Hints that his future was bleak and dreary, that brotherhood amongst this pack born in the wilds was an illusion.

That he'd been a *fool* for thinking otherwise.

Sickle's ears flicked back, teeth bared, his brow bunching over a scowl.

To think… what the prince meant to do him. To Renegade and any children she might bear… that he might be forced to set his claiming mark on the nape of his own—

Bile splashed against the back of his throat in a rush that surprised even him. And, turning just in time to avoid coating himself in sick, Sickle vomited a streak of sickly yellow that was dark against the red stone.

Heaving until his ears popped, he gagged and coughed. Ears drooping as he shivered on his quiet ledge.

"Fuck." He spat. Swiped at his lips with the back of one trembling hand, and spat again to free himself of that putrid aftertaste. His teeth coated with a layer of tacky filth that begged for a sip of water. For him to descend from his lofty perch and slake his thirst in the river.

But he resisted.

Unpacking his medical supplies, the slender male went to work. Laying out a strip of salvaged linen boiled clean, he smeared a spoonful of honey across the fabric. Spread thin, it was tacky enough to make a sprinkle of ground lichen stick. Enough to hold the assortment of various herbs topped with a fine layer of garlic sliced thin as he'd been able to manage.

And then, sucking a bracing breath through the points of his teeth, Sickle slapped it cold against his nape. Pressing it deep, he worked the poultice into the gaps between split flesh and ignored that it ached worse than the wounds themselves.

When the burning stopped, he selected another strip of sterile cloth and sealed the whole mess under it. Tied it off with a knot that sat at the base of his throat, then turned his gaze to overlook the camp.

To the place where Renegade had set her trap.

Where it had all gone so terribly wrong, and could only get worse.

He swallowed, head thumping against stone. Forearms braced over knees, he ignored the way his tail stump ached and throbbed.

She was lost.

Beyond all hope of rescue.

Bonded to a life-mate who would never return such a gift. Her undivided devotion meant for a *Hathorian* male. Not this... creature spawned by the Nine. A true juggernaut who could take as many females as he could entertain and never feel an instant of the ruin he would lay on Renegade's heart.

It was the Anhur way.

A polyamorous species who didn't form lifelong bonds.

And Giaus was the most gifted Sickle had ever seen—inside the Silver City and outside it. Such a beast could surely entertain a harem twice the size of Sinadim's. One the Sultans themselves would envy.

If the Trax didn't kill her, Renegade would *wither*.

Her enchanting fires extinguished in a bond that couldn't flourish.

Choking on the anguish, Sickle swallowed. Fighting not to think of that tiny, fierce queen locked away with the horrid beast she'd honored with her most precious gift.

Vulnerable and alone.

Sick.

With no one to tell her why any of it was happening. No one to guide her through such an intimate bond, but the animal himself.

He should have killed her in the clearing. Could have stopped her from marking Giaus with a single, well-placed blow, and given her freedom from the suffering she would be made to endure.

But now her misery would stain his hands just as surely as the ink twisting and curling over his fingers. The backs of his hands.

All of it, *his fault*.

Movement made Sickle glance toward the firelight.

Balkazar, the war chief moving at an alarmingly slow pace. One that weaved left then right and spoke of just how bad things were going to get.

Change on the wind.

And above it all, Sickle merely watched through eyes that itched with his grief. His self-loathing. Indulging himself with the notion that he might never come down. He could hold a vigil from here, watch until the camp was overrun with infected.

Enjoy the quiet for just a little longer…

Eyes burning, Sickle's gaze fell to his fingers. To the scattered medical supplies that needed to be prepared. Taking note of the things that needed to be replenished, he fished out a bunch of dried herbs and ground them with more vigor than could possibly be justified.

Worked until all that was left was a fine, silty powder. Until his tattooed forearms were burning with fatigue and the distraction fell second to a growling stomach. Long and whining. Protesting this hunger strike, but there he waited. Stuck between two paths—duty to pack or self.

Waffling between both, he sat above them all. Muscles cooling as the night wore on, utterly motionless until he could hear the distant, rhythmic rumble of sleeping males.

Snoring. The occasional grunt.

Eyes flicking toward the dying fire, Sickle sighed.

Balkazar was coming undone. That once-sharp mind of an Anhur war chief addled by the very same fever and infection that had turned Giaus into the thing that had upended their entire pack.

Struggling to stand, stiff and sore, Sickle straddled a choice. His loyalty to pack hanging by a thread, but it was one he himself couldn't cut.

If the prince meant to do this horrible thing, to take away the freedom he'd found in the wild and become a villain equal to Hadim himself, then he'd hear it from Sinadim's lips.

And if none of it was true? Merely the ramblings of a relic falling into madness?

It was what he owed to the prince he'd sworn a blood oath to serve.

A warning of things to come.

Hands braced on his lower back, right above the stump of his tail, Sickle stretched. Abs trembling as he reached, twisting left, then right. The vertebra cracking in quick succession of satisfying pops as he balanced on the edge of his quiet perch.

Deplete.

Heart sore.

Ravenous.

Descending with reckless speed, Sickle moved until he was close enough to the ground to let himself fall. To land on the balls of his feet just inside the mouth of Renegade's den.

He took a breath.

Slick.

It filtered through his brain and made his stomach twist in a painful, empty knot that hungered for more than just a scrap of food.

Fists clenched, ears pressed flat, he paused only long enough to allow his eyes to adjust to the gloom. To spot the single, hulking guard stationed at the top of the prison pit.

Sinadim.

His back to the light, the prince sat with arms crossed over his chest. Breaths slow and measured, he slept in the way of a common soldier—right on the edge of waking.

Sickle knew better than any just how dangerous it was to disturb a sleeping Anhur, and with the utmost care, he slipped into the dark.

Padding across red stone with bare feet, Sickle clung to silence. Oozing through the shadows, he gathered his courage in a comforting cloak. Stepped around any loose shale, and placed his feet with careful, deliberate intention, then skirted the rim of the pit. Positioning himself opposite Sinadim, with easy access to flee should this confrontation go as badly as it could.

Sickle cleared his throat. "Sin—"

A shadow fell across the mouth of the den.

Without thinking, Sickle dropped back. Hidden behind a large outcropping, his back pressed to stone, he crouched. Feet tucked beneath his thighs, breath held once more. His heart thrashing at the back of his throat.

For a moment, there was nothing but the sounds of harsh, ragged breathing.

A sniffle, followed by a wet cough.

Sickle twisted, peering through the gloom.

Balkazar.

Shoulders hunched, the war chief lurched toward Sinadim in a drunken line.

Face flushed, twisted and horrible, for there, in the dark, Sickle caught the sinister gleam of feral gold...

21

S inadim woke with a start, his senses returning in an instant of flushed panic. One-eyed gaze darting around the den, the prince bristled at the feeling that his space had been violated. Hackles going up, claws coming out, his attention snapped to the pit. Where he'd trapped Renegade with a monster in the cold, lonely dark.

Quiet.

The thatched roof of saplings woven into a lattice still intact. Untouched. His prisoners in their place.

So what—

"My prince," came a rough voice from the gloom. Garbled and wet.

"*Balkazar?*" Sinadim asked, shock making him jerk toward the sound in disbelief. That the presence of his most trusted ally had set him to such a state, his knees braced for attack. Squinting into the shadows.

The big male ambled into view. Shaggy hair hanging in limp clumps, Balkazar's head tipped to the side as if the whole world had tilted to the left. "I have news."

Muscles locked against the instinct screaming that he mount the first strike, Sinadim watched his war chief's approach. Gooseflesh spilling down his nape at the mere sight of the other male. Every inch of him *wrong*. From the shuffling, heavy footfalls landing without a hint of elegance or intention, to the way his claws extended and retracted. Pulsing in erratic waves that might have been a subtle threat, if it weren't for the flat and submissive mane. That the other's scent held no hint of musk or aggression, but was thick with a cloying film of rot Sinadim couldn't place.

Wrong, wrong, *wrong*.

The war chief's lips spread over a grin. "I understand what she meant."

Sinadim stepped forward, pacing to the right to keep Balkazar on his good side.

Snorting back a clump of wet, Balkazar horked, spat a wad of something green off to the side without bothering to blink. Not even once. "Thought at first it was more o' the same shit, eh?" he said, and jerked his chin at the pit. "Instead of having a warm quim at our disposal, we'd have to watch that lanky, infected fuck have his way with her." A burble of damp disgust tore free of Balkazar's throat in the shape of a laugh. "Followin' orders of the elite, made to play nurse and keep them warm and fed while we do all the heavy lifting? Thought, what's the point of all this, eh? Might as well still be in the Silver City, takin' it rough and dry from royal pricks who don't give a collective fuck about us at the bottom."

Shoulders still, Sinadim's mane stood fully on end as he tried to follow the bizarre daisy chain of logic. The quiet stink of pheromones filling the still air—his own, laced with uncertain fear. "And what changed your mind?"

Digging one clawed finger into his ear, the war chief shivered. Distracted as he itched, an audible *pop* echoed between brothers and Balkazar groaned. Tilting his head all the way over, his ear draining in a rush of bloody green slime.

Puss.

Reeking, putrid rot.

Relieved of the pressure, Balkazar seemed to rally. "Swore an oath," he said. Voice a distorted, gravelly rasp. "To protect the Karahmet line from any danger, no matter how insignificant. From yourself." Snorting again, Balkazar swiped at his nose, and left a slimy trail from the crook of his elbow all the way down to his wrist. "An' from worldly Omega wisdom," he chuckled, and grinned. "Remember that one girl we took from the Tengit uprising?"

Clinging to the wisps of his composure, Sinadim took another careful step to the side. Matched every one of Balkazar's movements. "I do."

Balkazar's eyes gleamed through a fog of recollection. "Took her until her heat ran dry, eh?" He thumped a fist to his chest. "Got her fat with one o' mine, too. Right beside yours." A misty smile touched the war chief's eyes, then. And he sighed, his mane flaring to a full stand before it lay flat and tame. "I shoulda been gutted for touching a bitch of that quality, but you gave me a shot at her womb."

Offering a placating smile, Sinadim said, "I remember, brother. She was to be your prize, when I took the Sultan's throne. A gift for your unwavering loyalty. The first omega in your own harem."

"You'll be a good Sultan, my prince. And..." Balkazar's eyes gleamed with an icy sheen. Glowing with an intense inner light. A veil of madness that set Sinadim's teeth on edge. "Wouldn't mind gettin' my knot milked again, eh?" the war chief hummed, circling toward the edge of the pit, he took a deep breath as he stared into the abyss. "She's not in heat anymore, our Renegade. But heard it's better when she's dry. Tighter. Less of a mess."

"Just the small issue of her declining health," the prince returned, and didn't blink as Balkazar exposed his back. He watched. Readying himself for the moment of reckoning that grew ripe on the vine. "Nothing can change that—"

Jerking, the other male spun. "*Change!*" Balkazar snarled as if he'd only just remembered why he'd come. Shaking his head, he flung droplets of ooze in a sweeping arc. "Can smell it on the wind. A new kingdom. A new throne."

Sinadim shivered, swallowing back the urge to distance himself. To set the other male off and draw more of Balkazar's fractured attention upon himself. "I don't understand," he said carefully, words slow. A soothing rumble.

Nodding, Balkazar staggered and slipped on a heap of loose shale, but caught himself before he fell. "But you *will*. It's the change, my prince. Don't you see? Wasn't meant for *him*."

Sinadim's breath caught, but he'd heard enough. "What are you suggesting?"

Arms spread, the war chief roared. "I feel incredible!" He sneezed and it was gummy enough that his forearm glittered with snot where he swiped at the slime. "That little bitch was *right*. It's a gift from the Nine themselves. One worthy of a prince, but she stole it. Gaping, vile whore"—Balkazar sneered, shoulders bunching, claws flashing a warning in the gloom—"all she wants is your seed, you know. Thirsty slut. Needs to be broken over a dry knot an' stuffed end to end. Like the old days. Two at once. Together."

"You're infected," Sinadim whispered, and it wasn't a question. There was no denying the scene unfolding before him. The horror of what needed to be done.

"Progeny instead of death!" the other howled, and lunged. Swinging a fist full of claws at the space where Sinadim had been standing only seconds before.

But the prince was ready. He didn't dip or dive—he lashed out with an elbow, and caught Balkazar across the brow. A spectacular strike that resulted in a bloody show.

Balkazar merely grinned, tasting himself

as his face was painted in a wash of shining red.

Retaliation was swift, the other male stocker than the prince. Muscle dense and meant for battle, where Sinadim was long and lean, he tucked his shoulder and charged with his head down.

Sinadim's knee stopped him short, cracking into the top of Balkazar's thick skull with enough force to stagger him. Lending the prince time to dance away, he skirted a large boulder on the far side of the pit—and stopped short.

Sickle.

Huddled in the dark. Staring up at him with wide, honey eyes.

"Fuck." If the war chief followed Sinadim's path, Sickle would die.

So Sinadim spun to keep the war chief in his line of sight. Stood between Sickle and certain death, motioning for the Hathorian male to move with a click of his claws, he watched Balkazar regain his feet. Watched him slip and land with one hand braced between his knees, and try again.

"Shouldn't be surprised," Sinadim drawled, pulling the focus onto himself with arms spread. Inviting the challenge with a smile that tugged on his scars. "Never figured you to be desperate enough to risk infection, but then"—the prince's smile grew sharp around the edges, taunting and cruel—"you've always been happy to lap up whatever cream I've spilled, haven't you?"

A low rumble raked over Balkazar's vocal cords, deep enough to be felt instead of heard. "You don't under*sss*tand, my prince," Balkazar slurred, and hooked his claws under the lip of the prison's latticed ceiling. He tore it free and sent himself tumbling to the loose shale yet again. Leaving the prison open, the pit a hungry yawning maw between them. "I'll show you, brother. From the source. You'll taste the Nine from the source—"

"Brother?" It was Sinadim's turn to laugh. "You're no kin of mine." Stalking closer, the prince held himself at the ready. His gaze sharp, assessing the fallen war chief with a keen eye. Waiting for that instant of opportunity he could smell on the wind. Fermenting as it grew near. And then, "I relieve you of your duty to the Karahmet throne."

Grant no mercy to the infected unworthy.

For a moment, Balkazar did nothing but stand there, heaving for breath. Winded. Shocked.

And then his icy blue glare flicked to the

opposite end of the pit. Flashed with a gleam of menace.

Movement.

Sickle, trying to escape the clash of giants.

Lurching, Balkazar launched himself around the far side of the pit. His movement jerky, lacking all finesse as he barreled forward. And in a clatter of loose stone and clicking claws, Balkazar threw himself between Sickle and the only way out. Panting through gaping jaws, he said, "No room for relics... that... can't adapt, eh boy?"

"He's older than you," Sinadim barked, and with one hand, he ripped Sickle off his feet and hurled him back. Into the safety in his shadow. "Run," he spat without bothering to look. His claws flashing, Sinadim caught Balkazar's flesh and tore open his chest.

A great shudder ran through Balkazar's heavy frame. His mane flickering across his shoulders, he paused. Swiped one hand through the coppery gore—then cupped his swelling length. "Can you fffeeelll it, brother?" Balkazar hummed, his voice utterly unrecognizable as the male he'd fought wars beside. "The Nine are calling..."

Sinadim rocked back, feet braced shoulder width apart. A huff of breath ghosted over his lips, but that was all the time he had before Balkazar lunged.

Clashing, the two Anhur met at the edge of the pit.

Sinadim caught Balkazar's forearms. Breath held, head twisted to the right, his blind side was protected. Straining for air that wasn't tainted by the corruption festering in Balkazar's blood, he gave Sickle all the time he might need to break for freedom.

"Yield," Balkazar rattled, his voice a rumbling coo that breathed terror into the prince's mind.

And with a snarl, Sinadim shoved with all his strength. Sent Balkazar stumbling back, while his claws sank deep into the feverish flesh of the war chief's forearms, Sinadim found an anchor. Leveraged his grip and spun the other male off balance.

With a wet slap, Balkazar hit stone. Dazed.

Sinadim retreated, tore his eye away long enough to watch Sickle's back disappear into the night, then said, "You know I have to do this."

Grant no mercy...

He stooped, fingers finding the sharp edge of a sheet of rock. A primitive blade. Lightweight, yet almost too heavy to lift.

Balkazar spat a gob of phlegm between his

knees, making no effort to stand. He gave up his back, chin tipped toward the ground. Hair hanging across his brow in sweaty, tangled ropes.

Feet heavy, Sinadim took a breath. "I'm sorry," he whispered, eyes fixed to Balkazar's thick neck.

And then, hefting his weapon high above his head, he swung.

Gleaming with an unnatural inner light, Balkazar's eyes slid over his shoulder.

Bloodlust.

It shone through a sinister grin. The spring to this trap.

Timing flawless, the war chief hurled himself clear of danger at the last possible second. Spun, and caught Sinadim's wrist as the blade struck stone. Leveraging himself to a full stand before Sinadim could so much as snarl or curse, he wrenched the prince's arm back and up. Not stopping until the joint popped and rolled out of the socket, he forced Sinadim into the wall hard enough to crush the very breath from his lungs.

"You'll see," Balkazar whispered, his lips moving against the prince's ear. Lined up, front to back. The press of arousal pulsed and nudged Sinadim's tail stump.

Wheezing through the pain, the prince snarled, "Get off—"

But Balkazar was far from finished. Hauling back, muscles stiff, he took Sinadim's captured forearm in both hands and spun his Alpha in a wide circle. Sent him hurtling toward the abyss on a joint that couldn't support itself. Relying on taut ligaments and empty skin.

Snarling, Sinadim flailed, lashing out with hooked claws, he ripped into Balkazar's cheek with his free hand. A lucky swing that bought him freedom, his feet planted on the edge of the pit. "Balkazar—"

He didn't see it coming.

The fist that sailed through his blind spot found anchor around the prince's throat. Fingers closing with force enough to crush.

But there was no fountain of gore.

No claws sinking into fragile cartilage, only the blunt tips of Balkazar's fingers against hot, sweat-slicked skin.

"It was always meant for you," Balkazar hummed, and Sinadim saw the eerie glow of infection ringing the war chief's pupil. "A gift worthy of a prince…" A smile ticked at the corners of Balkazar's lips. Choking, Sinadim spluttered, trying to break the other's grip.

For a moment, there was nothing.

Only the horrible sounds of wretched wet breath and the scrabble of feet against the edge.

And then, "The Nine wait in the shadows, brother. For you."

Sinadim tore free of the war chief's fingers, teetered, and fell.

22

Cheek pressed to lavish heat, Renegade indulged in the rumbling savagery of an Anhur purr. The gravely seduction she could no longer resist. Soaking up every precious note, each sound sung for her comfort, she hummed in tune with that perfect melody. Her mate crooning in such a way that she'd gone utterly boneless in his arms, liquid and pliant as the virus ravaged her insides.

Able to do little else but breathe.

And listen.

"Omega," he cooed, and took her fingers between his lips. Pulled them past his teeth where he laved those fragile digits. Tasting. Suckling as he uttered more of that hypnotic drone, he sent the vibration through muscle and sinew.

"Mmmm…" Blinking, she rattled and stretched. Her fingers plucked free with a succulent pop, she traced the bow of full lips. Watching as he kissed each knuckle, unblinking.

He pulled the fall of midnight hair over her shoulder. Careful claws dragging along her flesh, before he tucked his chin and pressed his lips between her brows. Eyes gleaming with golden heat, he caught her chin and said, "No other will give what I have given you."

As if awoken by the subtle reminder of what he'd planted within, her very core began to tremble.

The killing fever.

Spreading on the edge of a slicing wave of panic.

"Giaus," she mewled, twisting, her back arched as she searched for a sip of air not humid with the scent of infection. Swallowing tacky spit, her tongue swollen and thick with thirst. Forehead damp with precious, wasted moisture, she gasped. Tried to shake him off as a cold wave of nausea settled over her with a cold slap. "Giaus," she said again, the name rasped over broken glass and dry winds. Mangled by the Trax, she whined through chattering teeth. "I'm so… *thirsty*. It hurts…"

He nodded. Redoubled his purr, and watched as her eyes rolled back. "You are equal to this suffering."

Molten heat shot through her veins, and she preened when he stroked her from nape to hip. Arched into his palm and let him scratch behind the shell of both ears. His claws buried in the tangled mess of her hair where he worked at her scalp.

Leaking where she ached, Renegade gasped, lips working against salty skin. Her tongue tracing the dip and swell of a ragged scar on his chest. "Please," she rasped, and let her knees fall apart.

Needy.

Hurting.

So thirsty…

Giaus shifted, spreading her ass with the arm that supported her back so he might set his fingers to play at her weeping gate. Squelching in the slow trickle of fluids, his breath thrummed against her cheeks. Felt in the tiny space behind her eyelids, she was held in thrall to the raspy, hypnotic hum. "Tell me," he said, and fed her two hooked fingers. Drawing a patient circle around the base of her clit with the pad of his thumb. "What does my vicious warrior need of her mate?"

It was a simple question, but one that drew a ragged sob from her lips. One she'd never been asked before. Not by Hathorian or Anhur.

And so despite her thirst, she said, "You," as she watched him through the sparkle of unshed tears. Winding her fingers into the tangled mess of his knotted mane, she clung to a beast who snarled as he devoured all her little sounds.

Blissful agony.

It rippled through Renegade's body. Starting from the tingling ache in her overworked pussy, creeping out. To every soiled centimeter she'd never known to think about. Wanted and abhorred all at once, for her spine twisted against the over stimulation. Arousal drooling around Giaus' fingers while the killing fever wound through her blood and bone.

Remaking what she'd been into what she'd become.

"Don't—" Her breath caught, abs flexing as she tried to curl around the pressure building between her legs. A slow curve in, she hunched, inching closer to his heat, and said, "Don't... *don't stop...*"

Glaring, intrusive light splashed into their intimate dark.

With a throaty snarl, Giaus was on his feet. His arms wrapped around her ribs and under her thighs.

The comfort of his purr wrenched away, replaced by pure, unfiltered menace that bled from his chest directly into hers. Linked to a mate who couldn't feel her confusion, who issued a low, possessive growl and didn't see when her ears flicked back and her teeth flashed in the dark.

A perfect mirror for all that seething Anhur fury, both of them scowling up.

Territorial rage clouded his vision and hers, and Renegade's nape grew tight with a warning she couldn't broadcast without an emotive mane. Her every muscle wound tighter with each passing second, each insult traded from above.

Fighting between brothers.

Sinadim.

Balkazar.

Renegade blinked. Uncomprehending when the prince was forced to the edge of the pit at the point of Balkazar's claws.

When he fell.

Sinadim crashed into their prison with a snarl and a wet crunch. His ankle twisting at a funny angle before he thumped back. Skull cracking into Giaus' knees.

It happened in an instant.

Dazed, choking on stolen breath, Sinadim lashed out. Blind and confused, his claws caught Renegade's shin where it dangled over Giaus' forearm.

He pulled.

Too fast for her to feel anything, he unzipped her skin from knee to toes. Three and a half mangled, jagged slashes.

A bloodcurdling snarl spattered over Giaus' lips seconds before he sent a single well-placed kick into the prince's ribs and launched him into the wall opposite.

"Fuck—" Sinadim wheezed, then pressed his back to the loose shale. Wide, mismatched eyes fell to the damage he'd left on Renegade's flesh.

To the blood that spilled down her shin.

The little flaps of hanging skin.

His jaws snapped shut with an ivory clack. Face white, sallow and tinged with a shade of green that could be seen even in the murky gloom.

And without a word, the prince turned to face his end. Dragging his feet beneath him, Sinadim hauled himself up. Favoring one ankle as he clawed at the walls with only one arm—the other hanging loose and grotesque from a sagging joint. The prince flashed the white of his palm and let go a ragged breath, but that was all. Seemingly unable to form a single word, he said nothing at all.

Not a plea for mercy, or empty begging.

"You'll see," Balkazar called into the gloom from above. "Find it in the shadows, my prince. And we will rise, together…"

"You son of a"—Sinadim wheezed again, hacking up a gob of bloody spittle—"sperm gargling *whore*." A guttural snarl burst from Sinadim's lips, but he didn't dare to peel his eyes those that gleamed with feral madness.

Didn't so much as utter an apology or a single meaningless platitude.

With a reedy thump, the lid to their prison was hefted into place, plunging them into the dark once more.

The reek of rutting, territorial male mixed with the metallic tang spilling over her toes. And with a shuddery wave of black, seething hatred, Giaus dropped her behind his back.

Claws flashing, he surged forward with a snarl, bent on claiming justice. A charging wall of naked, bunching muscle, his tail stood high. Arrogant. A bristling signal that horrific things were coming for Hadim's son.

Injured, helpless but to brace, Sinadim grunted when they collided.

But Giaus was *everywhere*.

A giant beside the prince, he held nothing back. His fists landed in a flurry, both males shuddered at impact upon impact. Giaus lost to a territorial rage, the damp air was laced with choking pheromones.

With fear and murder.

Blond hair bled to crimson, Sinadim unable to land a single punch. His only working hand pressed to Giaus' sternum obliterated the careful kisses Renegade had placed there only moments before. Where his claws had sunk deep into that bronzed flesh.

But it wasn't nearly enough to save himself.

A plaintive, anguished cry was torn from Sinadim's lips. Crushed on a grunt before it could do more than reach across the prison— but reach it did.

Staggering, slipping on blood and slime, Renegade lurched toward that sound. Dizzy from fever and dehydration, drunk on Anhur fury, she swayed. Too short to worry about swinging elbows, she pressed closer. Tried to swallow a mouthful of dry ash, she approached from behind.

One ear tipped forward, the other back.

Delirious, she persisted regardless of the fever ravaging her from within. Reached with both hands.

"Giaus—"

His fist landed against Sinadim's cheek and sent the prince's head cracking back into stone.

Sinadim sagged only to be pinned in place.

"Giaus, *please*!" She coughed, her eyes burning and dry. Seeing nothing but a blur of dark, shuddering shapes. The hazy outline of males at war, her own pain forgotten in the face of such a blinding temper. "Wait!"

Feet bare, she trudged across their prison in three halting, blood-soaked steps. Her hands collided with Giaus' lower back, palms sliding against the sweat-slicked heat roiling off his skin. Hands slipping on muscle that jolted with every landed punch, contracting and heaving with the effort to kill the prince, Renegade found an anchor around the base of Giaus' tail.

She squeezed.

With a flick, Giaus jerked that fifth limb from clutching fingers and sent her staggering to the right.

Her knee buckled.

"Stay," he snarled, one wicked, gleaming eye cast over his shoulder. Meant to pin her in place, to force obedience while he decided her fate. And for a single moment, all that feral rage was turned back on her.

It festered and lashed, ripping into her chest with a cruelty she wasn't prepared to swallow.

He fed it to her anyway. Pumping her full, until her heart floundered beneath the weight of sick, possessive Anhur rage. A male defending his most precious possession against the one who'd damaged it.

She felt it all.

Nape tight, the muscles of her lower back bunched in unseen warning. Her ears flicked back, pupils constricted to tiny points of seething fury.

And still, Giaus felt *nothing* from his mate.

He turned back to Sinadim, drowned her outraged gasp with the merciless impact of fists on flesh. The hitching breaths of a dying prince.

Hadim's son.

Unbidden, furious tears flooded her lashes as the fever ravaged. Throat an aching desert, brain swollen inside her skull, she staggered to her feet. Fists curled into wicked claws where they were bunched at her sides.

"No."

The word trembled in the quiet space between clenched teeth. A denial, lost when she wrapped her hands around Giaus' middle. Set her cheek to that glorious heat, as his temper raged in her name... in her heart.

Renegade.

Bound to a mate offering things she couldn't comprehend, doomed to drip for the most dominant male...

... she was Omega.

Engineered to please. Forced to endure.

All she'd ever known was what Hadim had shown her. To submit and allow her life to be lived by the whims of another. The harem was as much a part of her as the killing tempest now running thick and hot through her blood.

Familiar and terrible blending with something... new.

Something... *worthy* of a name she'd chosen herself.

A thing starving for more from this life, to claim what she had earned.

She was the Renegade.

A queen.

And she would not be told to *stay.*

Sneering, she pulled a breath through her nose. All the way to the bottom of her lungs, where a painful swampy sort of wet had begun to fester.

And then she reached for her mate—not with her hands. Not seeking comfort of any sort.

No.

She strummed the poisoned dart he'd lodged behind her ribs. Pricked her finger and invited the storm into her heart.

Muscles coiled, Renegade snarled. Her eyes fixed to Giaus' profile, she flashed teeth filed short by a cruel master, and submitted to instinct.

Anhur instinct.

To subdue using any means necessary, any unfair advantage pressed without remorse.

Humming, a savage song of irresistible beauty flooded her mind. Gravely seduction laced with contempt for his species and their unconscious violence.

Her throat began to twitch.

Languid and delicate, a quiver of muscles never used before.

Sinuses full of an elegant, throbbing melody that bubbled up from the bottom of her chest. Muted on her next inhale, before that ethereal rattle spilled from the center of her being. Giving life on her breath, she sang to soothe a beast.

Her mate.

Giaus shuddered to a halt, the vicious tempest of swirling hatred suspended in an instant. Fingers that had been tight around Sinadim's throat went slack. The prince free to suck in a harsh breath as he slid to the floor of their dank prison. A boneless heap watching with one green eye. The other silver.

Staring at *her* in slack-jawed wonder.

She rubbed her cheek against Giaus' ribs, entranced by her own song. Worming her way under his arm, she burrowed deeper until she stood in the shelter of his embrace. Tracing the curling sweep of muscle over Giaus' hip, Renegade inhaled and set the air on fire. Felt his muscles lurch beneath her fingertips, a shiver that twitched in perfect sync with vibration pouring over her lips.

Lifting his elbow, Giaus looked. Face slack, he peered beneath the crook of his arm. His brows inching together on a wondrous frown, held rapt to her song.

Violence forgotten in the face of a sweet Omega purr.

Head tilting, Giaus stared. Speechless and unblinking, his pupils dilating in a slow sweep that swallowed the blazing ring of feral gold, until all that was left were bottomless pools of inky want.

"You will be king," Renegade said at last. His attention gained, she reached to touch where royal blood had spattered his cheek. His lips. Her voice heavy with the power to en-thrall Anhur males heated with bloodlust, be-cause it was their very same spell turned back on them. A mirror from her humble, Hathorian heart. "A king for the wilds. Out here, in a place that bows to you."

Giaus swallowed. Took a shallow breath through parted lips, and tasted the air. His tongue painting her scent along the roof of his mouth in that peculiar way of his.

Purring all the louder, she moved to sepa-rate them. Back pressed to Giaus' shivering abs, her palms laid to Sinadim's shoulders. The prince slumped at her level where he was sprawled in a puddle of blood, she stepped be-tween his thighs. Both of them bleeding, nei-ther in any pain.

Beyond it.

And through the drugging elegance of her purr, Renegade straddled Hadim's son and spoke to her mate. "You will be king, Giaus," she said again, and felt him drop to his knees at her back. "*My* king." A calloused palm wrapped around her ribs as she tucked her nose against Sinadim's throat—a warning is-sued too late. "But a king cannot rule without a general." She lapped at the Karahmet blood trickling down Sinadim's throat, shivering as the prince tried to escape her touch.

His chin tilting back, nostrils flared—his working hand landed on the curve of her shoulder. Neither pushing her away, nor pulling her close.

"But most important," she purred, ears laid low, a wicked smirk pressed to Sinadim's thrashing pulse, "a king needs his queen. And this choice is *mine*."

Before any might react, before either male could so much as shout a single useless command or dare to order her submission, Renegade lunged.

Blunted teeth sliced through skin and muscle. She forced her mark deep into that bronzed flesh—and with it, the virus.

It was a choice. One made through a fog of spiteful delirium, but a choice nevertheless.

Her purr fell silent.

And there was a price.

As if from very far away, she heard Giaus snarl, released from her thrall. Felt him try to wrench her away as the prince's clawed fist found an anchor at the base of her skull. Deadly points sinking in deep enough to score the bone, he held her there as she laid down a new mark.

A new claim.

The link in her chest writhed as if burned,

yawning wide before it split her right down the middle.

Renegade whined in exquisite, blistering pain as she was torn apart.

Her pieces divided between the Anhur.

23

S ilence.

It lasted only an instant. A single moment between the high, cooing purr spilling over Renegade's lips, and what came next.

Sinadim tried to twist and slipped in a pool of his own blood. Too dazed to feel the life-ending beating, the strained ankle, or the sagging, dislocated shoulder, he blinked and chased away the sparkle of dark stars. Trembling as a puff of soft breath caressed his throat.

And he knew.

What was coming.

Salvation from the beast, surrender to the slave.

Death on either side.

There would be no mercy for the infected unworthy.

His only chance to survive the next minutes, in whatever capacity that might be.

It was welcome, this ending.

A desperate, bloody capitulation of everything he'd ever known. The death of a prince.

Sinadim's eye flicked up, watery with pain. With everything else.

His chin tilted back.

An invitation and a denial.

Blind to both, Renegade struck. The imprint of blunt incisors slashed through his skin, and the claws of his working hand snapped to the back of her head. Held in a deadly cradle, he caught her there just as Giaus moved to tear her away.

A dainty snarl spattered against his nape and the female's jaw locked around her mouthful of flesh.

Giaus roared, hands moving to pry her free before the damage went so much deeper than bone.

Clinging to consciousness, Sinadim's claws found the base of that fragile skull. Did the only thing he could, laying there in a helpless puddle on the floor of a prison of his own making.

Piercing her scalp, he left marks on her skull. The point of one claw notched between the vertebrae an unspoken threat to sever her brain stem. And with a promise flickering in his eye, Sinadim met the rabid glare of a primal, frenzied male. Made sure Giaus heard the crunch of bone threatening to collapse under his grip.

"She won't... feel a thing," Sinadim rasped, slurring as he tried to shift and claim equal footing. To sit and meet Giaus' fury without having to stare up into eyes gone black.

But his heel slipped, and with a vibrated warning, Renegade's bite was driven deeper. Enough that her teeth caught and hooked at something vital, something that sent a shock through Sinadim's muscle. Made him twitch once before his arm went dead where it hung from the socket. Useless and numb.

"Kill me," Sinadim pressed, ignoring the injury to save his life, "and you'll kill her too."

Giaus seized Sinadim's throat in a calloused palm and squeezed. "You lie."

"Without her," Sinadim continued, letting his claws dig, "you won't last three days." Breath whistling through a compressed windpipe, he dared a smirk. "You need me, miner.

If you want her to live long enough to bear your monstrous fruit, you"—he coughed when Giaus moved to crush his windpipe—"you need me. *Alive.*"

"Lies," the brute spat. Eyes flicking back and forth, seeking answers across a landscape of scars, Giaus panted through clenched teeth. A mountain of fury held in check by concern for the tiny scrap of female flesh caught between them. "I am all she needs."

Fingers shifting in the tangled mass of Renegade's inky black hair, Sinadim's smirk became a grin. "Not anymore," he whispered, then swallowed against a palm that dared not call his bluff and seized his chance. "She's claimed a second mate."

With an ear-splitting roar, Giaus jerked that dislocated joint with a single vicious pull and laid Sinadim out flat. On his back in the middle of their dreary prison, a coveted female held fast in a lethal embrace—vulnerable as the beast searched for a way to pry them apart. "You think to take her from me, *boy?*" Giaus spat, and wrenched Renegade's knee up.

"I already have." Head spinning, his only focus the grip on Renegade's skull, on driving the other male past the point of reason, Sinadim laughed. "And there's not a fucking thing you can do about it now."

A growl thundered through Giaus' chest as the beast draped her thigh across Sinadim's belly. "You know nothing—"

"Oh? And how large was your harem, miner?" Sinadim returned, squirming when Giaus pressed down on her hips. Made him feel the liquid head of a Hathorian pussy melting against his abdomen. "Because I was a fucking prince! My harem the envy of all my siblings, bursting with too many Omegas to bother counting. I know everything you've never thought to ask about Hathorian females. Every weakness and secret strength. Every facet of their care a scrap of coveted information kept by generations of *my* forefathers. So tell me, king of the beyond," Sinadim sneered, intentionally goading the other male into a jealous rut, "what do *you* know of keeping Omegas?"

Giaus set his blunt tip against her folds, but chips of frigid obsidian grew ringed by a thin strip of burning, seething gold as his confidence began to crumble.

"You don't have to answer that," Sinadim whispered through a dangerous grin, and blinked at the bead of sweat that dripped into his eyes and couldn't be wiped away. Not with one arm useless and the other threatening to obliterate his new mate. "I know she's your first. Just as I know that without me to guide you, you'll kill her with ignorance long before she has another season. And for your failure, you will suffer unimaginable agony."

Renegade mewled against Sinadim's throat, dripping where she was wet and needy. Hips tilting back, she tried to present. Would have raised her tail in sordid invitation to be mounted and stuffed full.

Something sinister gleamed amber eyes, and Giaus said, "She sings for *me*," as he pumped his knob through a creamy mess and claimed her from the back in a single, punishing thrust. Fucking to dominate, to show Sinadim who was ruler here, in the dark.

That Sinadim was nothing.

But he didn't know the inner workings of a Hathorian bond. That it was a transaction, Renegade's part only half completed.

That it could still be undone...

"She pleads for a knot," Sinadim drawled, knowing just how it would provoke. "To be sealed by her mate—and now, *either* of us will do."

Breaking, Giaus' temper boiled over. Every inch the possessive Alpha, he snarled, "You will not have her!" as he sluiced through the flood of slick produced out of season.

Blindly falling into a powerful rut, at Sinadim's command.

Swallowing, hips flexing to relieve the tight, kicking brand of competitive arousal beating at his laces, Sinadim pushed all the harder. "She'll beg for me. Even as she cries for you," he said, shifting to feel the impact of Giaus' hips into hers. Each driving thrust bringing him closer to the edge, his voice hoarse with the thrill of taboo lust. "To deny her the attentions of a mate is a death sentence crueler than killing me here and now."

"FUCK!" Giaus reeled back with a howl of frustration. Planting one foot beneath Sinadim's ribs, he wound up and exploded. Punching the wall of their prison with force enough to turn stone into sand.

Unable to do more than squeeze his eyes shut as he was half-buried in the fallout, Sinadim focused on his grip. On the female saving his life by condemning it.

Protecting his leverage, for just a little longer…

Until it was permanent.

With a snarl, Giaus dragged them both free. Knees spread, he scowled down his nose with a purpose, adjusted Renegade's hips with a shockingly careful grip, and tilted her pelvis forward. Opening her for deeper penetration, so she might take all he had to give.

An electric shiver spiked up from the base of Sinadim's severed tail, tightening his sack as her pubis traced his length with every violent impact. Lewd to feel it this way, as a female might. Helplessly pinned, subject to the power of another's rut…

Teeth grinding, Sinadim crushed a desperate moan between his molars. Achingly hard, beaten and broken, but *throbbing* with need.

No matter the malicious contempt, the distaste for her kind, or that another male was about to make him cum.

Sinadim was drunk with a secret, obsessive want.

Utterly taken by the trilling sounds dragged from Renegade's throat—pressed against his thrashing pulse—as Giaus unleashed his frustration. Obsessed with the slide of shivering muscle as the other male drove him closer to climax. Utterly enthralled by the grip of a fucking Hathorian mating bite, where it was sown deep enough to unravel every conviction he'd ever held.

Shuddering, Giaus succumbed with a snarl. Buried to the hilt, he fucked an aggressive load into Renegade's cunt and made sure

Sinadim felt it—the kicking pulse, the rhythmic flex of heavy, swollen balls lifting so they might pump her full. And the stretch of his knot blooming so she wouldn't spill a drop of that virile seed.

Breath hitching, Sinadim dared a smile as a perverted bond was laid down between enemies. Set, sealed, and knotted by his own ignorance, Giaus himself bound them together.

It was done.

Back arching, Sinadim rocked into spilled slick soaking through his pants. That strangled groan breaking free at last, his cock lurched. Eyes rolled back. His dick kicking where he strained against Renegade's pretty, stretched pussy, his orgasm building—

One clawed fist darted between his legs, vicious talons that ripped through leather and nicked his sack. His balls caught in a nest of thorns, nearly pierced with a malicious violence that blocked the hot surge of cum before it might burst free.

Sinadim went stiff with a choked gasp, eyes bulging, abs flexing in horrified shock.

"You will be a puppet," Giaus rattled, his mane flaring around his shoulders, broadcasting his scent in an overwhelming show. Muscles working in a smooth glide as his pace wound down, his fist growing tighter.

Cruel. "Her eunuch. A useless fucking slave—"

"She"—Sinadim wheezed, bubbling and wet—"she can... feel... *everything*, miner. Mutilate me, if you want to torture... her."

"Foolish little prince," Giaus spat, twisting his wrist around that fistful of cock. Kinked at the base, he was held on the edge but unable to burst. Blood trapped in that stiff, vulnerable length. In his knot that had only begun to bloom. "There are so many pieces you don't need. Many experiments that can be run before I tear the truth from your broken husk. Pain can be endured," he hummed, claws needling into delicate flesh. "And Renegade is strong. She will endure, because that is what I demand of my queen."

Desperate for breath, Sinadim's head fell back. Vision blurred as everything went dim. Blurry. "Giaus—"

"Shhh," the beast hummed, and sweat dripped down his forehead to spatter onto Sinadim's dusty cheeks. He pumped once, fist over cock, and drew up a pained moan as Sinadim writhed on the edge. And then, hunching, Giaus folded himself over Renegade's back and whispered, "You don't have to die to give up your secrets. But you will suffer."

"You can't"—Sinadim groaned, tears leaking down his cheeks as Giaus worked him over—"can't undo it. Hate me all you want, but I'm not the one who—" He sucked in a breath when the giant squeezed, nearly shaming him right then and there. "You're quarrel isn't with me."

As if summoned to end it, Renegade stretched, humming as she let go her hold. Perverted work completed, she licked lips painted with gore. A satisfied grin tugged into place before her eyes rolled back, and she slumped. Sprawled between them.

Unconscious.

Oblivious to the war she'd started.

Breath caught, Sinadim blinked at the female who dared.

Entranced by the light, cooing snores that murmured against his collarbone. The lapping tongue that nursed at his wound.

"She needs... to drink," Sinadim rasped, and released his deadly grip on the back of her skull. Palm raised to show his surrender.

With a sneer, Giaus abandoned Sinadim's throbbing, bruised dick and claimed her limp body for himself. Settling back against the far wall, he tended the willful little bitch stuffed full of his knot. Checking her many wounds with all the frantic, obsessive attention of a doting matron.

And then, "I'm to believe you offer this… coveted scrap for free?"

"Self-preservation, miner," Sinadim said, uttering a ragged chuckle. He blinked and it was gritty, the honest truth spilling over cracked and bleeding lips. "Don't want to be trapped in here with you. When she dies of neglect and you lose yourself to a never ending rut."

Menace rumbled from Giaus' chest. A warning that went ignored.

"She needs to drink," he said again, and laughed, amused at his pale victory. At the cost of surviving what Balkazar was sure was a gift meant for the male who had been a prince. "More than either of us," Sinadim said, "she needs to replace what is lost in slick, or it was all for nothing."

Silence fell over the trio once more.

Quiet that dragged on and on and on, until Giaus' attention fell to the elegant creature cradled in his arms. A tiny queen.

His mate.

Theirs.

Sinadim could do little more than watch.

Breathe.

Bleed.

Suffer.

Fading in and out, he didn't move from where Giaus had left him. Cock hard and leaking despite the agony coming alive across every battered inch of his body.

He blinked…

… and couldn't lift his lids again.

24

She'd been quiet for a time.

Docile and still, while Giaus' purr flooded her senses and rendered her pliant. A drugging eloquence rife with a power he now understood. Knew what it was to be made helpless to the whims of another, to be broken down and made to watch, as if from very far away. Enthralled deeply enough that nothing else mattered. Not the pain of injury or the threat of loss.

There was only the next rumbling breath.

It was a tool, one he'd used to force Renegade through the worst of her feverish thrashing. The mewling, hiccupping pleading for something she couldn't name.

He purred when she kicked. Crooned when she shivered and moaned. Sang until his voice grew ragged and thin, the fire burning too low to keep her sedated much longer.

Time was running short.

But he hadn't slept.

And the only meager sip of liquid Giaus been able to procure had been for *her*.

Too salty and not nearly enough.

Not after what he'd done to defend his mate... the sordid depths he'd had to stoop to, just to keep her alive until he had the strength to escape.

To allow the other to live...

... to touch and quench.

Burning amber eyes flicked up and landed on the third occupant of this primitive prison.

Sinadim.

Skin blotchy and bruised, open wounds and abrasions speckling almost every visible stretch of skin, the other male had lost his battle with gravity. Slid closer while he'd been lost to the rest of the senseless, he was now crumpled against the wall next to Giaus' hip. Thigh to thigh, head lolling where it was cricked off to the right. Renegade's tiny feet tucked behind Sinadim's folded knees.

Entangled.

A possessive growl rumbled low at the back of Giaus' throat.

And for a moment, as he held a limp female close to the dry rattle in his chest, Giaus considered the many ways Anhur meat could be put to a better use. Here, in a place where not one of their wardens had thought to feed or water prisoners who couldn't go much longer without. But as he sat there, glaring, the flash of jealous rage faded as quickly as it had flared to life. Forced to consider the advice from a male who'd tasted what should have cost his life to know.

The warnings that they were linked, all three.

Bound together by a tiny female it seemed none of them could hold.

Not even him.

At least... not by himself.

An insidious whisper Giaus wouldn't have believed, if he hadn't seen her reaction to his wounds with his own eyes. If he hadn't used it against her, only hours before. The pain he felt left scrawled across her flawless brow, her fingers clutching at her side as if the spear had found an anchor between her ribs too.

But she'd claimed a second mate.

Taken on the burden of yet more slicing agony for the sake of an insufferable, spoiled prick who didn't deserve salvation. One who'd made threats grave enough to save his own life. Who'd teased at the depths of his knowledge in such a way that doused the urge to wreak havoc and spill blood, and earned him a respite.

Promising that without her, neither male would last three days. They'd fall to an ever-lasting rut that would end in unimaginable agony.

Giaus scowled at the other. Lips curled back, his scratchy purr became a hoarse growl.

There were more secrets to be wrung from Sinadim's mind.

But violence was an option none of them could afford.

A dull, throbbing pulse pattered between his ribs. Soggy where his wound was packed, the slow ooze of soiled dressings already saturated and spilling over. The promise of something ruptured while he'd rained fury down upon Sinadim.

Throat swollen and abused with over use, Giaus' purr stuttered to a halt.

Renegade's breath puffed against his chest.

A frown bunched between her brows. Nose wrinkling all the way up to her forehead, she squirmed in his arms. Spine flexing, ears flicked back, and as he watched, she whined. Low and keening, the sound of a wounded animal too sick to hide its suffering from predators.

He merely held her tighter, enough that her ceaseless shivering was slowed.

Not stopped.

And then blank, feverish eyes snapped open. Taking shallow, rapid breaths, she mewled and tried to sit. Tried to push her way free of his arms, becoming increasingly frantic as she fought the touch that had only moments before been enough to keep her tame.

"You need sleep," Giaus rasped, and petted sweaty hair back from her face. Trying to soothe. "The killing fever hasn't ended for you."

Renegade hiccupped around a sob, her ears flat when she burrowed deeper into his chest. Frigid, digging little hands found Giaus' armpit—her heels struck his packed wound.

Giaus recoiled with a hiss. Guts roiling, he adjusted Renegade's twitching limbs, and laid her flat across his lap.

Her head fell back, resting on Sinadim's thigh.

Keening, she squirmed and rolled. Pressing her cheek against the warmth of Sinadim's skin—where his shirt had bunched up at the back.

And then she stilled. Taking deep, huffing breaths against Sinadim's belly, her bones melted.

"She'll beg for me. Even as she cries for you. To deny her the attentions of a mate is a death sentence crueler than killing me here and now."

Temper fraying, *frustrated*, Giaus hooked extended claws beneath the collar of Sinadim's shirt—and split it down the middle. Giving her all the access she might need. To breathe as deeply as she might against the other.

"Wha—" Jerked from his senseless delirium, Sinadim woke with a start. Functional eye bleary with an over-bright sheen of glass, cheeks pale beneath the flush of a fever rampaging out of control. Forehead dewy, lips chapped.

And just there, on his shoulder... the crescent of Renegade's mark.

For a moment, as the two males made eye contact, Giaus was stiff. Bristling, the scent of pheromones broadcast his dominance across the small space. Every muscle locked, nape tight with the urge to assert himself above the other. To flex his status, tail raised in an arrogant sweep that left Sinadim with nothing. A destitute prince who'd fallen. Who now relied on the charity of a beast.

A killer.

But a moment later, Sinadim's mismatched

eyes rolled back, his head striking the bedrock with a dull thump. Lost once more. Harmless, declining further with every ragged breath, every whispered fragment of nonsense that crossed his parched and cracking lips.

Giaus went to work. Relieving Sinadim of his shirt, he tore the fine, worn linen into strips and saw to Renegade first. Wrapping her calf tight enough to force the ragged edges of flesh to meet, he bound the damage done to her shin. Four slashing claws that had flayed her almost down to the bone.

An accident already paid for.

Nose pressed close to her skin, Giaus lifted that slender leg and inhaled, searching for the scent of infection. Tongue painting the roof of his mouth, so he might taste any hint of festering rot.

What he found made his mane rise up in a slow, shocked halo. Evidence that his mate, this precious Renegade Omega, was so much more than he'd ever thought possible.

She was *pure*.

In him, the Trax virus was a sour, toxic thing. Reeking of mutation. Of havoc and madness that worked horrific change at random—in him, size, speed, strength, and limits he had yet to push. But in the beast that had infected him?

Giaus shuddered.

Pressing his nose behind Renegade's ear, he tongued the spot where her scent was rich and intimate, her flavor bursting across his palate. Behind his eyes, where she danced in his brain. Lit by shimmering colors, she was burned deep inside him.

Where he could taste the change unraveling in her blood.

In her the Trax had become something more.

Something new that reeked of potential. Of stable balance.

His eyes flicked back to Sinadim, to the imprint of her teeth set in a half moon high on his shoulder.

And he wondered what she would be, this tiny queen he would keep.

With a grimace, he stood and draped Renegade across Sinadim's chest—to protect her against the chill of damp stone.

It was a disrespect. To use the other male by paying him no mind. Treated not as a rival, but a pacifier for his mate.

Only when she was settled, did Giaus dare to unpack his own wound. Pulling the prickly lichen from the hole where the spear had been, he caught the scent of fermenting garlic.

Sweet and sickly, but not the reek of festering meat.

And there, peeking out from the limit of his vision, the edges already pink and warm with new growth. His mutated body trying to make light of so grievous a wound.

Still, gore spilled over his hip. Sluggish, but pulsing with a surge of fresh blood.

Grinding his molars, Giaus stuffed a wadded bundle of linen into the pocket between his ribs. Trying to stop the bleeding before it pooled inside. One hand pressed to the rough shale, his tail tucked between his cheeks. Sucking tight breaths through thin lips, he replaced the package of healing herbs and laid his palm over the wound.

A tiny sound drew his attention back to his mate.

Pain. Renegade squirming on Sinadim's chest. One hand kneading at her ribs where a phantom ache throbbed and writhed.

He swallowed, and gleaming amber eyes slid over the curve of her back. Where Sinadim's only working arm was wrapped around her middle.

Mismatched eyes glared back from the dark, Sinadim roused by the fussing. His brow damp with miserable sweat.

"She can… feel… everything, miner. Mutilate me, if you want to torture… her."

Lips peeled back, Giaus pushed off the wall. Kneeling at Sinadim's side, he wrenched that shoulder back into the socket with a squelching crunch, and said, "Speak."

With a gasp, Sinadim writhed in place.

But it was Renegade who sighed, her brow smoothing out as the source of her discomfort was lessened.

"Tell me everything you know of Hathorian mating bonds," Giaus grated, and slipped both hands under Sinadim's armpits. Propping him up against the crumbling shale, before he reclaimed his mate. Sat back against the opposite wall of the prison, his tail tucked as he cradled Renegade against his chest. "Leave nothing out."

Glaring in the dark, Sinadim merely flexed his fingers. Claws extending and retracting, he tested the function of his repaired shoulder.

But said nothing.

Giaus smirked, taunting. "She means for you to be a general. *My* general," he rasped, voice reedy and faltering. "You spoke once of unity. Of marching side by side as we take vengeance on the Silver City."

Sinadim's lip curled. His fingers moving

up, to prod at the bloody ring of Hathorian teeth set into his skin.

"I have no interest in the wars of weak males swaddled in luxury," Giaus drawled. "There is far more to be gained as the ruler of these wild lands. Where the Nine breathe life into their chosen few."

"Trax," Sinadim said, and scratched at his claws until they came away wet. "A plague of the unworthy."

"There are things out here you cannot imagine. Dangers spawned from the ashes of our ancestors, fed by the fools who throw Anhur over the wall." Giaus' mane flared. "Fools you know better than any."

Blinking, Sinadim slung one arm over his knee, and said, "Make your offer, miner."

"An alternate proposal," Giaus hummed, his smirk a wicked thing. "One that puts you second only to me."

"A general."

"Of a feral army." Grinning, Giaus wet his lips and tried to relieve the strain on his vocal chords. "Lend me your secrets. March at my side and conquer a kingdom far greater than any you meant to inherit."

Sinadim's eye flicked to the female curled in Giaus' lap. The question went unspoken, hanging thick enough to taste.

But for a long while, he didn't seem to so much as breathe.

"I have to piss," Sinadim whispered at length, head thumping back against the wall of their prison. Wrinkled brow a direct contrast to the soft laugh that passed his lips. "Insufferable cur haven't left us a shit bucket, have they?"

In spite of himself, Giaus snorted.

"I…" the prince swallowed, throat giving up a dry click. "I cannot hold it any longer."

Jerking his chin toward the lowest point of their narrow cell, Giaus pulled Renegade more fully into his lap. Greedy for her weight pressed to his skin.

Swaying, Sinadim stood. Claws fully extended, he clung to the walls for the two paces it took to gain what little privacy he could. The muscles of his low back bunching and flexing, shivering where his tail might have displayed his pain and irritation. His discomfort.

But he'd been docked, and Giaus was left only with the presumption. The memories of what his own experience with the Trax had been.

For a moment, Sinadim was silent except for the wheezing breaths of one who'd spent too much energy on so trivial a task. Shoulders slumped, one forearm braced against the prison wall, he waited with damp brow pressed into the crook of his elbow. The other hand wrapped around his cock. Mane limp.

The sound of rushing liquid preceded a hiss of pain, and the fist that wasn't between his legs pounded against the wall. "Ah, fuck," he choked, and the stream of urine came to an abrupt stop. "I'm pissing blood, miner. By the Nine, that hurts."

Another pathetic trickle eked out, but that was it. And when the prince returned, he was dappled in a fine sheen of sour sweat that was heavy on the palate.

And then, "She shares your pain," he said without turning. "Your rage and joy. Everything. I didn't realize… I'm not sure what a dual bond might mean for a Hathorian."

Eyes locked on the ceiling of their prison, Giaus' thumb traced the edge her jaw. "And this bond… it's a one sided thing?"

"If only," Sinadim rasped, and turned to slide back to the granite floor with a grunt. "It only makes sense to start from the beginning." He sighed, then. Head tilted back, feet slipping against the bedrock. A helpless gesture that saw Sinadim's cheeks flush with heat, as his ankle pressed closer to the giant's warmth.

Giaus didn't react. Not when Renegade

whined—reaching again for that something intangible—and not when a bit of loose shale crumbled from the edge of the pit above, scattering them with falling debris.

"They're a weakness we can't resist." Sinadim coughed, misting the air with the coppery scent of stale blood. "Wars are fought for possession of fragile creatures that need constant tending. Countless Anhur sacrificed for the best Hathorian bloodlines. The larger the harem, the larger the hybrid armies that march forward in their father's name. All of it for slick. The pinnacle of Anhur luxury," Sinadim said with a dry chuckle, his eyes sliding closed. "The addiction of choice amongst royalty"—he coughed again, spat out a glob of bloody spittle—"for its ability to cause a powerful rut. Ecstasy at a whim. I was no exception. Addicted, as are any with unrestricted access. Breeding a large harem is endless work, but it's the only way to feed the addiction without the risk of a pair bond."

Giaus frowned, peering down at the tiny thing draped across his lap. The female that had brought him so much. "Seems easier to take one, instead of dozens."

Nodding, Sinadim fought to remain sitting. "No more rebellions started by desperate males with no options..." Trembling, he propped himself up, knees tucked high and tight. Braced against the slippery floor, he made to take the higher ground. Tried not to touch the massive male who'd beaten him senseless with a nauseating ease. Failed. "Only a bonded Omega can produce slick on a whim. No more waiting for her heat to ripen. But there's a price for unlimited access to such a rare nectar," Sinadim wheezed. "And when a commodity is scarce…"

"Horded by the elite?" Giaus hummed, doing little to hide the contempt.

Sinadim shrugged, accepting the accusation. "Pair bonds are a tactic used by the skin traders. Those with enemies they mean to control. To punish." He blinked. "I've seen it myself. Obliterated nests of bonded Omegas rented out to any who can pay. Slick on tap, one female can service dozens in a single day. They lead short, horrific lives that end in brutal deaths. Broken over a thousand knots. They're wretched creatures," Sinadim whispered, his gaze dropping to his claws. "For them… death is welcome. A mercy."

"And the Anhur they're bonded to?" Giaus asked, combing Renegade's hair as she slumbered in his arms.

Mane bristling, Sinadim bared his teeth

around a savage grin. "Doomed without their bonded Omega. Condemned to an everlasting rut, they fuck themselves to death. Unable to knot or cum. They spend their last hours paying the price. Mindless beasts searching for an outlet that doesn't exist, they'll use any hole they can. Male… female… enemy or friend. It doesn't matter. Endlessly rutting until the body breaks down and the heart comes apart. That's what she's done to you. *To us*. If that girl dies," Sinadim said, shivering sweat bloomed across his brow, "we won't last three days. And if we can't find a better way to hydrate her? Less."

To this, Giaus had nothing to say. Nothing to offer but a tight nod as he gazed at the creature who'd killed them both.

"So," Sinadim said. Sniffling, his mane bristling on a shiver he couldn't suppress. Lips quirked. "King of the beyond. How long do I have? Fever and chills I expected." He jerked his chin toward the ceiling of their prison. "But Balkazar is showing all the traditional signs of the infected. Rotten idiot that he is. How long before I succumb? Before my brain is filled with puss?"

"Are you frightened, prince?" A savage grin split across feral teeth, glinting in the gloom. His lips parted, tongue flicking up, to paint the roof of his mouth in her scent and bask in what only he knew.

"I'm not a prince," Sinadim returned, and shifted to the left. Crossing his ankles, knees spread, his toes brushed Giaus' shin.

The giant's glare flicked to the contact, but he said, "And I'm not a miner. I was a smith before I became a king."

Head tipped back, a laugh huffed over Sinadim's lips. "Well that explains your deadly right hook." And then, in a voice that trembled, "How'd you survive it?"

Taking a breath against Renegade's temple without once letting his disturbing gaze slide free of Sinadim's face, he pulled her closer. A mate he'd have to share, despite the urge to soak his hands in Sinadim's blood, but smeared across his palate?

The secret truth that was all his own…

Legs falling apart, his gaze flicked up. Toward the light. "Luck," Giaus said, and that was all.

Sinadim followed Giaus' gaze.

But here he would wait. In a hole, trapped in deplorable conditions, with flimsy security totally insufficient to keep one such as he locked away in the dark.

Waiting. For his wounds to heal. For his mate's suffering to ease…

For the winds to shift, so he could rise from the dark with a queen at his side. His general on the other.

A conqueror for the wilds.

The mutant king and the half-blind prince.

It was nothing less than what she deserved. What she'd asked for, in claiming them both. To be worshiped by two males named mate, her primal needs serviced. Appetite for rebellion nurtured by a male who would see her rule—her vicious instincts honed to a deadly point by the other. Males who would feed her wildling heart to bursting, her thirst quenched by more than just what might be pumped down her throat.

Her every savage whim satisfied.

Until she begged for more...

25

S printing through the night, Sickle fled. Seen only by the watchful gaze of triplet moons sitting fat and lazy on the horizon, where they peeked through the canopy and bore witness to his greatest shame.

Haunted by his failure. By the sounds he'd heard echoing up from the bottom of that pit, in knowing that he'd been too late.

He'd never forget the echo of fists on flesh. The horrible snarling yelps of a vicious beating silenced too soon.

The prince was dead.

A victim of Balkazar's madness, Sinadim had taken the full weight of Giaus' territorial rage.

But with his fall, Sickle's oath was no more. His obligation to the Karahmet line expired with the end of the prince.

He was free.

No queen to serve. No master to obey. No allegiance to brothers who wouldn't act, except to save themselves.

Alone, for the first time in his life.

With a hiccupping sob, Sickle vaulted over a fallen tree, his pack of medical supplies slung over his shoulder where it bounced freely at his hip. Racing along the river's edge, he darted through the shadows. Unarmed. Eyes flicking back and forth with the sort of vigilance he'd learned in the Anhur courts. He fled knowing it wouldn't be long before Balkazar noticed his absence, until he was hunted down and made to answer for his daring. To pay for breaking his vow to his brothers.

Balkazar meant to finish what he'd started down by the river.

But even knowing the war chief could track his scent—that he was faster, stronger, and had more endurance than Sickle could ever dream of wielding—there was a chance. A possibility that Balkazar was too sick to hunt efficiently, and no matter how unlikely his survival, Sickle had to try.

For her.

Knees buckling, Sickle collapsed. Palms slipping on wet stones, pebbles slimy with algae, he went to hands and knees. On all fours. Heaving for breath beside the peaceful trickle of the river. The same one they'd followed in search of a precious Hathorian female in heat, drawn to the irresistible lure of slick in the water.

Tears spilled over his lashes, dropped from the tip of his nose and fell to the detritus. Left the leaves dark and speckled with his grief.

A female of incomparable worth, Renegade was a treasure many would die just to touch.

And by the Nine, *Sickle had touched!*

They had all tasted that sweet slick and known what it was to transcend the horrors of their life in the beyond. Just for a moment. Just long enough to be utterly ruined by it.

This was the price of such daring.

He knew that now.

Didn't regret anything, except failing to save her from a fate so much worse than death.

That he could have been the one to give her a merciful end, but wasn't.

Sickle scrubbed at his tears, took a breath, and forced himself to stand. To move, because he *couldn't* save her. Not from Giaus, not from slavery to a predatory species, and not from the Trax.

It was too late.

Renegade was lost.

Mated to a beast.

And now, in honor of the one female he would have served joyously, Sickle would never kneel again.

Teeth clenched, ears pressed flat, he abandoned all he'd ever known and charged into the river. His satchel held aloft, water swirling around his chest, he was cleansed of the stink of fear. Washed clean of everything but the inky swirls of his past. A clean slate he could fill with his own etchings.

Panting, Sickle paused to listen on the far bank. Alert for the sounds of pursuit.

He was not disappointed.

"SICKLE!"

It was a roar of primal fury, his absence noticed already. Anhur wrath trumpeted through the trees, thick with outrage that saw a half-mad grin stretching over Sickle's lips.

That Sickle would dare to save himself?

A dire insult to the racial hatred that defined so much of Balkazar's existence.

Sickle's advantage, for he'd spent his time in the wilds learning from the Anhur, but they had not done the same. They'd taught him to fight like an Anhur, to hunt and kill and fuck like an Anhur, but not *once* had they looked to the Hathorian in their midst and seen anything but a helpless burden.

A weakness.

Something lesser than.

Grinning, Sickle's ears flicked back as he heard the far off sounds of the war chief crashing through the woods.

He spared nothing for panic.

Merely adjusted his satchel and steadied his breathing.

And then he ran.

The pain of his injuries forgotten.

Flitting from one shadow to the next, he flew through the woods. A phantom unnoticed by predators both large and small. Following a trail he didn't know, he went where his instinct demanded. Not moving as quickly as an Anhur might, he clung to efficiency.

Muscles hot with effort, he bolted for the light in the dark. Where he might be seen by the triplet sisters and bathe in the pure, white light shining from those lunar monocles.

Strides long and sure, chin tucked and ears flat, Sickle gave everything he had—and found the well deeper than he'd ever believed possible. The world blooming all around him, rife with possibility. Bright, despite the late hour and the moons.

He whooped, flashing the point of his

teeth. Grinning as he darted between the trees.
Over rocks and through the brush. Wild.

Free.

A dull, animal lowing caught his attention.
The humming drone of too many feet to count.
An army on the march, thundering in the same
direction.

Sickle skidded to a halt at the forest's
edge.

Scanning the clearing, he saw barren, dimpled hills of limestone. Pocked and dented,
void of anything green or lush, it was a net-
work of tunnels that wormed deep un-
derground.

And just there, in the distance?

The rising cloud of an approaching horde.
A mob of infected, both mutated and
grotesque. Beasts without Giaus' sharp wit, or
noble measurements. They were horror
trapped in flesh. Doomed creatures cast out by
the Nine.

Demons who ate without bothering to kill.

And he was standing directly in their path.

Sweat bloomed over Sickle's nape, his
forehead growing damp and clammy as he
watched them approach. Sneering at the mindless terror urging him to flee, he glanced back,
toward the way he'd come. To Balkazar and
the cruelty he knew would end him.

This was a choice. A fork in the path between two options—return to the life lived for others, or to be swallowed up in a single horrific instant. Pummeled to death beneath the savagery of a feral horde.

Death on either side, because Sinadim couldn't help him now. The hybrids wouldn't bother.

There was no one left to save him.

"*SICKLE!*" the war chief called again, closer now. Balkazar's skills as a hunter had not been diminished by the infection rotting him from the inside.

And then Sickle saw the horde in a new light.

Salvation.

A tool.

Sickle chose a new way. One not manicured by the cruel influence of others.

"What a pretty justice," he cooed, grinning into the shadows. Searching for any hint of Balkazar breaking through the tree line, he hunkered down to wait. To set a trap for the war chief who meant to be an Alpha, who'd taken *everything* from him but hadn't been made to pay the price.

Yet.

When the distant crashing of a beast grew

loud enough to pick out each individual foot-
fall, Sickle sprang into action. A moving target,
he sprinted and claimed the ground halfway
between the limestone summit riddled with
dark caves and the forest. Arms spread in welcome when Balkazar burst through the trees.

Eyes rimmed in red, oozing from every
orifice, Balkazar looked wretched. His bulk
seemingly increased in uneven waves, his
right arm hung heavy from the socket. A club
of muscle and deadly claws more wicked than
any Sickle had ever seen.

Dripping in all manner of horrors, Balkazar's brow was furrowed in dim confusion.
Sensing the trap, even in his state, he hesitated. Not yet seeing the danger rolling toward
them, there was time to taunt.

Time Sickle meant to use.

Grinning, he said, "I have to hand it to
you, war chief. I was wrong."

Balkazar's head tilted. Heavy and distorted
on one side, something noxious and green
spilling from his ear.

"You've adapted to this place better than I
ever might have expected." Grinning, Sickle
took a single, calculated step back. "You have
purpose, relic. Still expendable," he said, and
shrugged, "and your death will be heinous, but

it's a fitting end for a diseased whore like you."

Mumbling nonsense, Balkazar's mane rose up in an uneven flare. The pounding of a balled fist into the opposite palm was enough of a clue about his meaning.

Sickle laughed, just to keep those watery blue eyes focused on him. "You took everything from me, and now it's time to take your reward. And I have to admit," Sickle shouted as the horde drew near, "I'm going to enjoy watching you fall. They're going to dine on your flesh and knot your every ruined orifice, but you're meant for this." Sneering, Sickle took another step back. Drawing Balkazar fully into the barren stretch of limestone. "Only this."

And then, bellowing challenge, Balkazar charged.

Limbs working as fast as they might go, Sickle raced the front edge of the horde. Bathed in a moonlit shroud, he claimed a cloak of confidence that might earn him a grisly end, but would do so at his own authority. That would take Balkazar down with him.

Tripping over limestone, Sickle's boots snagged on uneven ground. And he leapt, clearing the desolate, barren planes of rock and spewing geysers puking up sulfurous smoke. Vaulted over a pool of bubbling muck rimmed in crusty yellow foam, and staggered over the bulk of a massive beast.

Dead.

He spun, just in time to watch Balkazar skid to a halt exactly where Sickle had paused to taunt. The danger noticed soon enough to avoid being swallowed by the horde—but they turned as one hive mind nevertheless.

Roaring, a writhing mass of festering rot between them, Balkazar sent one last searing glance at Sickle, then retreated.

The horde followed him into the wood, back... the way he'd come...

To a clearing of red stone beside a quiet river. A void in the forest where a queen had been born and died.

Where the male who'd been named Sickle had fallen with her.

Sinking into the shadows, he let go a trembling breath.

And laughed, ribs heaving. Unable to muster any more sorrow, even knowing what the horde would do to the pack he'd once been bound to serve. To the hybrids who wouldn't act... and to the mutant king who'd doomed a precious queen.

Eyes flicking over the corpse of a lava-kin, he braced for any hint of threat as the horde ambled on by. Nudging the beast with the tip of his boot and saw the carnage. One of the most deadly creatures living in the beyond, its jaw had been nearly torn from the skull.

Frill limp and broken, its chest was sunken and cracked. Bones poking through a thick hide that no longer shimmered with white-hot flames of divine fire. The eye sockets were hollow and yawning where something small had burrowed inside and eaten every last morsel of brain matter, much of the meat picked clean. The skeleton still smoking, bones charred black from the heat of a creature born from the blood of the Nine themselves.

And there, beneath scales and bone...

... *movement.*

The corpse twitching and writhing with life.

He staggered back, tripped in a pit burnt into stone, and went down at the mouth of a cave. Shocked and staring.

A tiny face poked through scaly skin. Two gleaming eyes bisected with an alien slash of inky hatred blinked up at him with an angry little coo. Head tilting with a sharp click, a minuscule frill snapped open an instant before the little thing was surrounded by siblings.

Lava-kin clutchlings.

Eating their brood mother down to the bone.

Swallowing the nausea, Sickle turned to slink into the caves—a warbling tri-toned cry pierced his ears, and was mimicked by the rest of the wryms.

Ears flicked back, the Hathorian male hissed. Showing teeth. "Not by you lot," he sneered, crouching in the shadows as the horde grew ever nearer. "Not today."

Fanning out, the clutchlings squealed more of that high-pitched sound that sank into his chest and vibrated in the jelly behind his eyes. The largest of them shivered—a tiny female with her bright red frill and muted speckles that would one day glow with white-hot heat. Her chest pulsing with a fragile, immature blue light.

He couldn't help the smile. Felt a certain type of connection to a creature he could squash beneath his heel, who stood guard over her siblings and threatened to wreak havoc in a fight she couldn't win. Who reared back to balance on stocky hind legs, dancing a warning that would only be terrifying when she outweighed any Hathorian and could spit vomit hot enough to cremate.

But that day hadn't come.

Earth rumbling, the last of the horde vacated the clearing. Moaning and retching, the unfortunate lost brought the reek of putrid, mouldering flesh.

Obliterating the scent trail of one lonely Hathorian male wandering the wilds alone…

Grinning, he ignored the fragile predators, darted into the mouth of a cave, and found himself in a tunnel warmed by thermal vents. Narrow enough that he was made to crawl, he breathed through his teeth to avoid the stink of reptiles left hanging in the dank, still air. Panting as he moved deeper, his senses primed for the slither of something heinous lurking in the dark.

At his back, a shadow jumped to follow, and the male whirled. Ready to fight to claim this scrap of quiet peace, as a fallen prince had once taught him to do.

A body rasped against the loose shale on the floors. One, followed by five more. Tiny things, trying to be large.

Glowing brighter where the moons weren't, he could see the poke of bones through tender hides…

… and realized too late what starvation looked like…

Out here, in the wild beyond, monsters roamed. Eating their meals raw… without bothering to make a kill…

Thank you for reading Giaus, The Feral Court Book II. Were you rooting for Sickle throughout this book? Good news! That feisty Omega male is coming back with a vengeance in the next installment of *The Feral Court!* Read Sickle today!

If you like *free things, sneak peaks, giveaways, and super secret news about future projects*, then boiii is there a place for you! Tis called The Daniverse, and you can join by searching for "The Daniverse, by Myra Danvers" on Facebook.

MYRA DANVERS

USA Today Bestselling author, Myra Danvers, is best known for her compelling mix of unique science fiction and dark fantasy worlds that feature feisty heroines, antihero men, and of course, proper villains. Though you may not always know who is who until the final pages…

Join The Daniverse:
The Daniverse, by Myra Danvers

Visit her website:
MyraDanvers.com

facebook.com/MyraDanvers

instagram.com/myradanvers

bookbub.com/profile/myra-danvers